D1707619

© 2021 Copyright David Lady

Imprint: Independently published,
Ocala Florida, USA

This is a work of fiction. Any resemblance
to actual events or persons, living or
dead, is entirely coincidental.

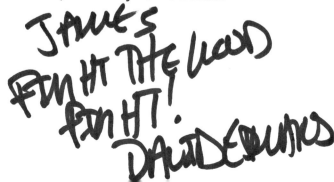

THANKS
FROM AT THE NICE
! THINK
DAVID ZUNIGA

AUTHOR'S NOTE

The first time I was in a firefight was in Panama eight months after basic training. I was then, and am now, probably one of the least likely people to get angry in any situation; it just isn't a big part of my makeup.

Even back then, though, I was a student of human behavior, so I observed everyone on my team carefully. I was just a private at the time, so it really wasn't 'my team', but that's how I thought about it.

Anyway, there seemed to be two emotions present at first enemy contact. Some people got scared, some got angry. I naturally assumed I would be one of the scared ones and mentally prepared myself to fight through the fear and do my job. But that's not what happened.

Instead, I was one of the angry ones. More than angry, really, furious would be a better word. The emotions provided clarity and focus that I have rarely achieved or needed since leaving the military.

Another interesting experience of a firefight that surprised me was the sounds. There were four primary sources of noise: friendly fire reports, enemy fire reports, friendly chatter, and the sound of the incoming rounds, which sounded like bees.

This last noise was new to the moment, only present during the real thing. It was just the weirdest unexpected buzzing sound.

Of course, in basic training, we had done live-fire exercises where they fired actual rounds over our heads while we ran an obstacle course. But in the real world, having someone shoot at you sounded a whole lot different than having someone shoot over your head in training.

I was also surprised at how fast everything went. Almost the exact opposite of books and movies, at least in my limited experiences. Many people I talk to tell me, for them, time slowed down. Not for me; it sped up.

At any rate, a few insights into why the 'action' in *Panama Red* is described the way it is. Different than traditional book thriller 'tropes' where the fight scenes go on for dozens of pages. I just don't remember it that way.

I hope you enjoy reading *Panama Red*. I very much enjoyed the process of writing it.

- D. Edward

SYNOPSIS

During what was supposed to be a routine low-level investigation in Panama City, Panama, US Army Special Agent Dirk Lasher finds himself embroiled in a power struggle instead: Caught between Noriega's militant police force and a mysterious organization planning to use Panama's banking infrastructure to crash the international financial markets with the goal of a new world order. Ultimately leading deep into the murderous jungles near the Panama-Colombia border, a deadly race of discovery devolves into a primal fight for survival.

If you are a fan of Brad Thor, John Sandford, or Tom Clancy, you will love this new pulse-pounding adrenaline-filled adventure by Amazon Best Selling author David Edward.

OTHER BOOKS BY DAVID EDWARD

Westerns:

Alamosa

Science Fiction:

Reason
Ancient
End of Reason
War Machine
Unreasonable
Oldtech

Military Thrillers:

Panama Red
Stormfire (2022)

PARKING LOT

US Army Sergeant Jack Williams parked his car outside the old condo high-rise on the Bay of Panama. The day was crisp; sparkling blue water in bright sunlight as a warm wind pushed the ocean's salty smell inland.

Williams wore his preferred attire for fieldwork, a tacky Hawaiian shirt, and shorts.

As he got out of the car, two men approached. He hadn't noticed initially, which meant they had been concealed somewhere. It wasn't that big an area. They were dressed in PDF uniforms, the Panamanian Defense Force, a combination of police and military that Noriega used to run the country as he saw fit as dictator.

"Friend, would you please step away from the car?" one of the two officers yelled in Spanish, advancing.

Williams watched them both; they each had a sidearm in a holster on their belts. The one who spoke rested his hand on it as police did worldwide to be on the ready. Not an aggressive stance, but one that suggested he already had the drop on you.

"What's the problem, officers?" Williams said back in English, not stepping away from the car. His overnight bag, federal badge, and sidearm were in the back seat. They had caught him before he could open the back door to grab the rest of his stuff.

Panama, under Noriega, did not have the same concepts of due process and civilian rights that Americans were used to. There were no Miranda waivers. The justice system (if that was the right name for it) was suspended earlier in the year, mid-1987, under a declared state of national emergency.

Both PDF officers, stepping apart, continued to move forward, reaching in unison like a choreographed dance, removing the snaps on their sidearm holsters. Glock 30s, .45 ACPs with thirteen-round magazines.

Good solid weapons.

"Fellas," Williams said smiling, putting his hands in the air while looking around, surveying for additional threats or options, "what's this about? I've got to get ready for our New Year's Eve party tomorrow; that's no crime, right?"

Two more officers materialized from the other side of the parking lot, now working their way forward.

Williams considered his options: fight or flight. Neither seemed viable.

He stepped away from the car, hands in the air, searching for any advantage, becoming frantic to find a way out.

"*Turn around,*" an officer said, now a pair of handcuffs in his hand, getting close.

Williams couldn't find an option.

He turned, feeling sudden movement as soon as he did, whipping his head around just in time. The officer without the handcuffs was nearly on him, in the process of taking a running swing at his head, hard. Instincts took over, dropping his leg, intercepting the blow, rolling the PDF officer with his momentum across the bent leg and onto the ground.

If this had been single combat, Williams could have delivered a killing or debilitating blow, in total control of the contest. But it wasn't. Suddenly he had the other officer's Glock pressed into his face along with a lot of frantic screaming in Spanish, the two other uniformed men breaking into a run toward him.

"Okay, okay, everybody relax," Williams released the downed officer and put his hands back in the air.

The blow came from behind him; sunlight suddenly turning pure white.

Then nothing.

MEXICO CITY

Kimberly Sharp was the most influential person in Mexico, but she could have been a ghost. Very few knew she existed, fewer what she did for a living. She wasn't famous, didn't own very much herself, wasn't a politician or an actress. Her official title was benefactora—benefactor in English. Spanish required the identification of gender in the title.

She was the brainchild behind the Global Bank Group, the GBG as it was called. She wasn't the CEO or president or even an employee. She didn't own any stock or have any legal control.

She was its *benefactora.*

The GBG existed as a means for her to exhibit influence, and it did what she told it to do.

From time to time, she would teleconference into a board meeting. Rarely she might need to send a courier directly to the GBG CEO if he were heading into the weeds or doing something else stupid. She mostly had enough spies and operatives through-out the organization that she only needed to tell Hernando what she wanted, and he got the word around.

Hernando was her messenger in the same way that God sent angels to deal with humans. She spoke, and Hernando delivered God's word to whomever she directed.

If she were happy, Hernando made it rain happiness.

If she were unhappy, Hernando made it rain hell down on whoever had displeased her.

Today she was unhappy. If she didn't do some-thing to change her disposition in the next couple of hours, she would need to skip the New Year's Eve party tonight. She would be in no mood for it.

The sun was setting, long shadows on the deck of the penthouse slowly cooling everything off. Mex-ico City had excellent weather this time of year: mid-seventies during the day and the fifties at night.

Sharp sat at her deck table in a padded chair. She wore an expensive white business suit. Her eyes were an icy blue, piercing if she looked at you. If you dared to look back into them, you noticed that her eyes, while bright, were more like doll eyes. There was some piece of human empathy missing from their return gaze.

A strong breeze blew today. Sharp loved the wind out on the penthouse deck. It cleared the layer of pollution out of the city, allowing for good visibility. From the top of her high building, she could just see the Pyramids of the Sun and Moon several miles away, in the distance across the large metropolis that was Mexico City. The wind made the view better and created a sense of excitement, feeling dangerous this high up.

Two businessmen were on their knees in front of her. An hour ago, they had been seated at the table, drinking sparkling water, providing her an update on the Panama project. The project had fallen behind schedule, they said. Unforeseen obstacles, but they were working on it, they told her.

In return, she motioned for Hernando. He had his men pull the two from their chairs, beating them, but not too much. Cutting their expensive suits off, not being overly careful, the knife digging deeply here and there in the process.

But not too much.

Hernando was an expert at just enough.

He had a graduate degree in it from the school of hard knocks. An ex-special force's officer in the Mexican military now in his early forties, having led many raids into Guatemala from Mexico as those relations deteriorated earlier in the decade.

Sharp wiggled her finger back and forth, making a show of selecting one of the two men. She got great excitement from moments like this. She felt a warmth that settled in over her providing great pleasure.

Maybe I can salvage the party tonight. Yes, I know what will help.

There was nothing better than watching the life strangled out of a subordinate. It never got old, being the commander of death, making choices that changed the world forever. The trick was to keep eye contact and wait for that moment just before it was over when the struggling stopped and resignation set in.

That fleeting millisecond of knowledge of the coming transition, then gone.

She spent hours wondering where they went. It kept her up at night. When young, she had experimented on animals. Now she could experiment on people.

Strangulation was the only means she had found to produce the proper, well, post-mortem "effect." Each victim always came around after death, providing her the postmortem physical reaction that she found uninteresting with the living.

Once they die, they love me unconditionally.

She selected one of the men. He had been the project manager. Before he could protest, Hernando had the man's belt around his throat.

"*Wait!*" Sharp yelled, leisurely getting up and walking to stand pressed against the man, looking face-to-face, close enough that their bodies were touching.

She watched his eyes; they were dancing around with fear. He was trying to talk, his tie shoved into his mouth, preventing anything other than grunts and gurgles.

Without blinking, being careful not to miss it, she took a deep breath, feeling that building excitement, smelling the fear in the air. "*Do it.*"

Hernando tightened the belt; the man struggled. She could feel the moment coming. Feel his body spasming against hers as his life flowed away.

There it is.

A flash!

There was a moment of electricity, then he was gone, the eyes lifeless and rolling away.

What did he see?

She continued to stare at him.

Tell me! I know you can hear my thoughts!

She stepped away, beginning to shake, her head spinning.

Hernando let go of the belt, and the man fell to the ground, crumpled.

Sharp swooned, then sat back down. She took a moment, looked at the other businessman, his eyes wide in disbelief, darting left and right like a panicked deer.

Looking back to Hernando, she said, *"Take the live one inside and get him cleaned up. When he is himself again, remind him that we don't fall behind schedule at the GBG. He has a week to get the schedule back to what we agreed."*

Hernando nodded as one of his men pulled the man to his feet.

As everyone started to leave, Sharp called out, *"Hernando! Roll this first one on his back and give me an hour of privacy,"* she said lazily, still in the afterglow.

Hernando did as he was asked, just like always, not thinking anything of it.

BACK ALLEY

L asher ran as fast as he could, waving his arms, signaling *Over there!* He hopped over trash cans and piles of junk and garbage as the backs of the houses flashed by. The alley ran the whole street behind the houses, unkempt, as much trash dump as a thruway. Buzzards were here and there working through the garbage, paying Lasher no mind.

Two Panamanians ran fast on the street in the same direction, covering the area in front of the houses compared to Lasher in the back alley. They and Lasher caught glimpses of each other between each house, quick flashes of movement. Both the Panamanians were younger, mid-twenties at the most, with long hair and a rugged look to them.

There was a black flash. One of the Panamanians leaped over a front-yard fence, the other grabbing a pole to help slow himself down. Lasher saw it between houses and tried to stop himself, overrunning by several dozen feet. He paused, breathing heavy, then sprinted back the way he had come.

There was a commotion and the sound of bottles hitting concrete. Lasher grabbed a burlap sack off one of the piles of garbage as he ran by, now carefully advancing down the small gap between houses connecting the front and the back.

"*She's coming your way!*" someone yelled in Spanish.

Lasher saw her, low and fast, running right at him. He opened the sack and waited, jerking left as she approached, forcing her right. He moved with practiced precision, falling with the bag open onto the ground at just the right moment.

"Got her!" he yelled, victorious.

The sack was adjunct panic, thrashing about, small soft growls of displeasure. Lasher wrapped his arms around it as best he could to keep the burlap from tearing, careful not to apply too much pressure to cause an injury to himself or the baby panther.

He rolled over, sitting up, the sack in his lap, his muscular arms wrapped around it. The little animal was strong. The panther calmed down. Eventually, he allowed it to pop its head out, careful to hold on, so it did not escape. The small animal's blue eyes were taking Lasher in, looking around actively.

Thomasito, one of the two Panamanians, walked

up to him. *"Don't let her go!"*

"I got her," Lasher assured him, petting the cat's head, causing it to meow at him and pull its head away.

"They're cute when they're little," Thomasito said.

Lasher agreed. *"How did she get this far into the city?"*

Thomasito looked back, away from the Bay of Panama and north to the jungle, the bay two miles south and the jungle two miles north. *"Happens more than you would think. It's fun when it's a little one. Once fully grown, that little cutie will kill you in under ten seconds. Two hundred pounds of hungry jaws and claws."* Then he turned to Lasher with his hands out, suggesting Lasher hand the cub to him.

Lasher started to, then pulled the animal back. *"Tomas, you're going to release her back into the jungle, right?"*

Thomasito feigned a look of insult. *"We Panamanians are civilized, friend. Only an American would even think to do something else."* He saw that Lasher was unconvinced. *"Of course, old man."* He yelled over his shoulder, *"Julian, bring the car around! We caught her!"*

Lasher made a face at the "old man" comment as he handed the cat in the bag over to Thomasito. He was only a few years older than Thomasito. "Have you ever encountered a large one? In your short time so far on the planet, that is," he added, referencing the old man comment. The cat's claw nicked his arm as he let go of the bag, drawing a small amount of blood.

Thomasito took the cat and scratched it behind the ear. "No, they are rare around the city. But if you go into any of the deeper jungles, you are almost guaranteed to encounter one. They will stalk you for hours before attacking. Very dangerous. We'll take her about a mile in and let her go. It's not far."

Lasher nodded, waiting for the car with Thomasito, waving as they were loaded and pulled away. Once gone, he looked to get his bearings and was surprised at how far down the alley away from his house the chase had brought him. He started to walk back up the alley, then thought better of it; it was pretty disgusting in places, so he made his way around to the main road through the front of the neighborhood and started the walk back.

Even the front of the neighborhood looked worse than it usually did today, and it usually looked pretty bad. Not as bad as the back alley, but the trash and remnants of last night's New Year's Eve parties were still ever-present.

Goodbye, 1987. Hello, 1988.

A smell seemed to be following him. He smelled his shirt; it stank like garbage and sweaty panther cub. He would have to change and shower when he got home, which was fine. He could clean out the cat scratch at the same time.

His house was in a derelict neighborhood in a worn-out section of the sprawling urban cesspool that was Panama City, Panama. The area was called *El Cangrejo*. It had once been a good neighborhood, but not anymore. Street gangs ran things now, providing the only authority. The gangs were not overly organized and easy to deal with if you showed respect and didn't interfere with their business. Probably more on the up-and-up than if Noriega's PDF were in charge here.

All the families that could move away from the neighborhood did so long ago; most couldn't. Panama was the paradise that wasn't: rampant poverty painted against glass-tower high-rise luxury. Two worlds, each unmindful to the other.

El Cangrejo, the name of the neighborhood, meant "the crab." No one knew why this name was used for this area, but it always had been. Lasher joked with Thomasito, from whom he also bought home-brewed beer. Lasher called him Tomas, a good-spirited nickname he adopted for the guy. He told Tomas that *El Cangrejo* sounded to him in English like "the kangaroo."

Thomasito didn't think Lasher was funny or care about what *El Cangrejo* sounded like in English. But he was happy to sell beer to the American at four times its street price. He also liked Lasher; the man had charisma for sure. Everyone in the neighborhood enjoyed having Lasher around; actions like helping save a baby panther cub would endear him to the locals that much more.

As Lasher walked back, he noticed rain clouds to the east in what otherwise was a clear sky. In Panama, there were two seasons: wet and dry. It was just at the end of the transition now, heading from the wet season into the dry season, still plenty of rain, but less each day. The sunsets looked the same here as in Miami, where he grew up, bright sky colors against lush green foliage and clear blue water.

Raised by his grandfather after his mom died when he was eight, he had grown up in Little Havana, just outside of Miami, Florida, USA.

Grandpa Lasher had been a tail gunner in World War II, shot down and spending the last year of the war in a German prisoner of war camp. He hated the show *Hogan's Heroes* (even though he watched every episode) and always had a dog named Fritz for as long as Lasher had known him. It wasn't always the same dog, but it always had the same name. Grandpa would get frustrated when people thought he served in the Air Force during the war. He was an Army man; the Air Force didn't exist back then—one more newfangled inconvenience.

When Lasher got back to his run-down house, he went inside, grabbing one of Thomasito's beers from the refrigerator, opening the bottle cap by twisting it off. It wasn't meant to be a twist-off, but the press they used wasn't very good, so it came off easily. He walked out the front door and sat down on his front step looking south in the direction of the Bay of Panama. Since south was the direction his house faced, that was the way he looked when he sat on the front porch.

The setting sun was to his right. He could see the sun but not the bay from here. He knew the bay was only a few miles away because he could see the tops of all the modern high rises built on its shores in stark contrast to the look of the local surroundings.

His grandpa would have had some derogatory name for the bay, something like "the tyrant's swimming pool" or "the vulture's dumping ground," only using more colorful words. Grandpa liked to swear a lot. Lasher idealized him as a child but decided when he was twelve that he would never use a swear word again, a mishap at school, his first awareness that home life and social life had different rules.

Lasher watched his grandfather live out his final days using this exact model—sitting on his front step buzzed by morning, drunk by noon when he would take his naps.

Lasher finished one beer and opened another. He had a decent buzz himself, just at that perfect place where you felt good, but the headaches and indigestion had not yet set in. He was at that beautiful point where you wanted to feel this way forever and knew if you could just get one more beer, you might be able to pull it off.

Grandpa would have called this feeling breakfast. Lasher smiled to himself, enjoying the memory, feeling pretty good.

Lasher's black hair was in a ponytail, pulled back and tied with a woman's hair clip.

Somehow it made him look tough.

He hadn't shaved for about a month nor bathed in a couple of days, but he needed to desperately now, putting it off as sheer luxury because he could. He was undercover after all and had to clean himself up at least once a week. The Army, in its wisdom, required even undercover agents to come in to post once a week for a "deployment status meeting."

Even unwashed, you knew when you looked at him that he could carry his weight. No matter how much awful beer he drank or how long he drank it, his eyes always had a spark in them. He tried to hide it, but it was there.

Thomasito knew it was there, as did everyone else in the neighborhood. They figured Lasher was some type of undercover CIA agent. They were not too far off. Thomasito fed Lasher small bits of information. Just enough for him to get paid, not enough for him to get in any trouble.

The Americans were always active in and around Panama City. They had bases west and north of the city and oversaw the Panama Canal, the eighth wonder of the modern world. There were growing hostilities between the American soldiers and the PDF. But the PDF didn't come around here. There was no one to pay them off and too much trouble with the local gangs.

As Lasher sat there on his front porch step thinking about his grandpa, he noticed two men approaching his house. They both wore long-sleeved Cubavera shirts; one man's shirt was yellow, the other man's shirt was blue. Other than that, they could have been brothers. They were tall for Panamanians, looking more like American Indians than the indigenous Guna or Naso peoples that lived in this area.

As he watched the men approach, he put his beer down, leaning back against the middle step, feeling for his 9MM handgun pressed against his back where he wore it with a modified holster he had made himself. Only it wasn't there. It was still inside. It was a magnificent handgun, a Springfield XDM, a prototype he managed to procure from a company bidding to supply the new handgun of the US Army. It was still two full years before it would be in mass production. Unlike standard-issue Beretta M9s, the XDM had a nineteen-round magazine, four more rounds compared to the M9.

It was a heavy gun, but it shot almost as well as a

rifle. Lasher wished he had it on him now as these two looked like trouble. The two men approached with confidence and arrogance, surprising as they were from outside the neighborhood; these were not local thugs.

The one in the yellow shirt spoke first. "*You understand Spanish, gringo?*" he said as he walked up the short walkway between the sidewalk and Lasher's porch. He spoke in Castilian Spanish, the common language of the civilized Panamanians.

Lasher had dealt with plenty of tough guys growing up in Miami, Grandpa Lasher even sometimes making him fight older, bigger kids.

He looked up at the men from the middle step. "*A little,*" he returned in Panamaji, a street combination of Spanish and English. It would be the dialect most expected from an American ex-pat. Lasher spoke seven languages and many dialects of Spanish, but that wasn't important at the moment.

The other man, blue shirt, spoke next. "*We're looking for a friend of ours.*"

Lasher kept watching the man, waiting for a response, but that was all he had to say. The wait grew long, so Lasher put his hand down to push himself up to a standing position. As he did that, the one in the yellow shirt pushed him back, forcing Lasher to slip awkwardly and land back where he had been sitting.

"I didn't tell you to get up, *el tonto*," he said to Lasher in mostly English.

Lasher made the fall look more awkward than it was, but he was not wholly faking; he really was a little drunk on the beer. After reseating himself, he looked up to the guy in the yellow shirt who had pushed him. While maintaining eye contact, he made a gesture to the other man in the blue shirt.

The guy in the yellow shirt said, "What?" It was a forceful statement.

"*I found your friend,*" Lasher said in Panamaji, pointing again at the other man. "He is right there. *Allí,*" he said using English, then the Spanish word for *there* at the end.

Whoever these guys are, it looks like the one in yellow is going to take a swing at me, he thought.

He could sense the strike long before it happened.

The man in the yellow shirt swung his arm to slap Lasher in the face. It was going to be a hard hit, and it would have stung. The edges of Lasher's buzz immediately fell away, and he was stone-cold sober in the moment; dipping his head to avoid the swing, he saw it coming from a mile off.

He was willing to remain passive to continue his undercover work and see where this went, but only just.

Anger replaced the calm of the alcohol buzz.

Yellow Shirt smiled, missing with his swing. Waving his arm now as if trying to dismiss an unpleasant smell, which in all fairness, he was, Lasher smelled worse than the neighborhood at the moment, and the beer hadn't helped.

"*That's not him?*" Lasher said in Spanish with an edge but smiled.

If they make another move like that, I am going to take them down. I hope these guys are not related to the locals, but I can't sit here and look weak.

He noticed several of the neighborhood residents had come out to see what the commotion was about. Thomasito and Julian were walking back from parking their car several houses down on the other side of the street in front of Thomasito's house. It was impossible to read their expressions; Lasher could not tell if the gang knew these two outsiders or if they did not. Deciding it didn't matter either way, at this point, he was not going to take another attempted slap to the face or any other act of aggression. He put both hands up as if to say *Enough!* Then he slowly put one hand down to push himself up again.

The man in the yellow shirt raised his arm, making a show of it, suggesting that if Lasher stood up, he would smack him.

Lasher continued getting up; Yellow Shirt took the second swing.

Tired of it, Lasher moved quickly, sweeping his leg under the man, moving expertly, almost too fast to see, extending his right hand into the man's solar plexus as he fell, slamming him to the ground while propelling Lasher to his feet.

The man hit the ground hard, his head slamming into the paved walkway. He was down harder than Lasher had intended, blood starting to flow from the back of his head into the unkempt yard.

The man in the blue shirt was surprised but recovered quickly, reaching behind his waist, presumably for a handgun.

Lasher saw the move, continuing his motion from the other attack. He spun his back leg around, raising it high in the air. His heel connected with blue shirt man's face with the full torque of the spin. Lasher felt the crack of Blue Shirt's nose, blood splattering out in all directions from the blow.

Blue Shirt fell to the ground yelling obscenities in English, holding his nose gushing blood, a thick stream flowing to the ground and forming a puddle under him.

Lasher returned to a ready position and looked out to the street, not knowing what to expect. He saw Thomasito and two other guys walking over to him. It was not a threatening walk. Their postures seemed to show genuine concern.

"Wow, man, you move like lightning for such an old dude! Who are these guys?" Thomasito asked Lasher when he got within earshot.

Lasher looked at Thomasito, then down to the two men, *"You don't know*?" Lasher said. "They asked me about their friend from last night but didn't give me any more details. It was like they thought I should know." Lasher started in Spanish but finished the thought in English.

Thomasito reached down and took the wallet out of the back pocket of blue shirt man, who had his head down and backside up in the air. His nose was no longer gushing blood but was still bleeding. Thomasito took out a wad of cash, put it in his pocket, and then took out the driver's license. After looking at it for a long moment, he handed it to Lasher.

"Americans," Thomasito said.

Lasher took the license, looked at Thomasito, then at the license. It looked like a Panamanian driver's license to him. "This looks legit to me; why do you think they are Americans?" he asked. Lasher had been breathing hard from the exertion; he was recovering, his breathing returning to normal.

Thomasito smiled. *"See the staple?"* he said, pointing to the tiny staple holding the man's picture underneath the lamination of the license. There was the smallest amount of discoloration present.

The staple was rusting.

"See the rust on it?" Thomasito said. *"Real licenses from the DMV use galvanized metal. The ones your American agencies make use of are regular metal. It's*

a legit license, but the rust tells me it came from the American Embassy or one of your bases."

Part of the treaty with Panama allowed the American agencies to create real driver's licenses and Panamanian government ID cards, which they did. Lasher knew his license would have the same tell.

The thought must have crossed his face as Thomasito smiled at him. *"Don't worry, friend, we know you are an agent too. But we like you."* He waved his arm, indicating the neighborhood in general.

Lasher smiled and made a friendly "you got me" face, then looked back down to Blue Shirt, who was starting to recover.

Thomasito punched Blue Shirt in the back of the head hard. The swing came from nowhere, not the sloppy telegraphed slap Lasher nearly took earlier from Yellow Shirt. The blow knocked Blue Shirt out, his face landing on the walkway in a pool of his blood.

"He's gonna feel that tomorrow," Thomasito said, shaking his hand after the impact.

CLEANER

L asher called the MI contact number at Corozal, where the in-country US Army Military Intelligence (MI) S2 resided. The US Army was divided into commands. Inside those commands were G and S hierarchies. G represented the general staff, and S the executive team. In this case, S2 was the organizational intelligence and security component of SOUTHCOM, the US Southern Command.

Thomasito sat on Lasher's couch, watching him as he made the call. Yellow Shirt and Blue Shirt were tied up slumped on the floor against a wall in the room—two of Thomasito's friends, big guys, standing near them, watching. The two suspected agents were still unconscious, although they could be pretending, so no one was taking any chances.

Lasher waited on the line. Finally, a new voice responded, "Go."

"Lasher, six-seven-five-six," he said and waited.

The line clicked a few times then a female voice answered, "Go," with the same inflection as the prior voice.

Lasher knew who he was talking to: Captain Janice Crostino, the current company commander of Bravo company in the 470th Military Intelligence Brigade. She was Lasher's commander; he reported directly to her. She ran about twenty agents in the field at any time and had another forty soldiers in field support roles in an office building on the nearby army base.

"I need to know who two US government agents are," Lasher said. "I have the names on their Panamanian driver's licenses. I believe they are using their real names. Let me know when you are ready."

Lasher snapped his fingers at Thomasito a few times, pointing at the two licenses Thomasito was holding, who leaned forward and handed them to him.

There was a pause on the other end, presumably Captain Crostino getting paper and pen. "Go ahead," she finally said.

"The first one is William Walker. The second one is Soon Citlai, Charlie-India-Tango-Lima-Alpha-India." He handed the licenses back to Thomasito.

"Give me a couple, and I'll call you back." The line went dead.

Lasher sat down in an oversized chair across from the couch where Thomasito sat. He looked over at the agents, then back to Thomasito. "How long have you known I was undercover?"

Thomasito smiled, speaking surprisingly good English. "*My amigo*, every six or seven months, a new guy shows up at this house, lives here for ninety days or so, asks a bunch of questions, pays for information.

"You all look the same, like soldiers who grew their hair out. It is a running joke here. But you pay me fifty bucks once or twice a week, and you pay four times what we charge others for beer. And you, amigo, drink a lot of beer."

"Does it bother you?" Lasher asked. A thought occurred to him in the moment.

Every six or seven months?

"No, we count on it. A US presence here keeps the PDF away. Whatever you are doing, you never interfere with our business. We like the USA much better than the PDF. So, we do as you say: let bygones be bygones."

Lasher laughed. "I think you mean live and let live."

"They don't mean the same thing?"

Lasher thought about it. "Close enough, I guess."

One of the bound men started to moan. It was Blue Shirt with the busted nose. The man did not look good; he was pale, blood caked in his black hair and on the right side of his face. His nose continued to seep blood, creating two red streaks down from his nose and onto the front of his shirt.

Thomasito looked at his two men, then back to Lasher. "You wanna let him wake up? *He doesn't look so good.* Another blow to the head to knock him back out might kill him."

Yellow Shirt started to moan but didn't wake up, the head wound might be worse than Lasher thought.

Lasher didn't want to interrogate either man until he knew who they were. He looked at Thomasito. "*Can you send someone for some duct tape or something?*" He said it in Spanish so that Thomasito, who nodded to one of his men who ran out, did not have to repeat himself.

A few moments later, the man returned with silver duct tape. It had dried blood on it, stuck on the edge and inner cardboard. Lasher pointed to the blood on the tape, and Thomasito shrugged his shoulders to suggest he was shocked to see it and had no idea how it could have gotten there.

Lasher shook his head, then nodded to the two prisoners. "*Make sure they can still breathe, but wrap the tape around their heads a couple of times so they can't talk*," he said in Spanish.

The man with the tape did as he was asked, wrapping it over both Yellow Shirt and Blue Shirt's mouth and around their head a couple of times. Lasher noticed he went straight around. It was going to be hard getting the tape off where it ran through their hair. It suggested the gang's skill was in the application of duct tape, not its removal.

The phone rang; Lasher answered. It was Captain Crostino on the other end. "I have an emergency brief for you. Williams should have stopped by two days ago on his way to his assignment to deliver you the challenge-response, sorry. It says that two DEA agents with those names will be contacting you. The challenge is *'we are looking for a friend of ours .'* The response is, *'we are all friends here, amigo.'*

"Does that help with anything?"

DEA meant that these were Drug Enforcement Agency operatives. Lasher thought about a sarcastic response but then just landed on, "Yes, ma'am," an easy military close.

He hung up the phone. "These are DEA agents. *They're friendly*."

Thomasito looked at Lasher quizzically. "We saw them take a couple of swings at you. *How is that friendly*?" First English, then Spanish.

Lasher had worked with the DEA several times before. Just like these two, they tended to be arrogant field agents. Lasher always felt they had a chip on their shoulders. Every DEA field agent he ever met either didn't make the cut to join the FBI first and settled on the DEA or talked endlessly about how they would transfer to the FBI after just a bit more field experience.

"*Cut them loose, please, and get the tape off their heads before they fully wake up*," Lasher said as he stood up and walked over to the window. "Tomas, I am supposed to be gathering information on drug distribution here in Panama City. Crack, Panama Red. The only reason I didn't interfere with any of your business is that you don't run drugs here in the neighborhood."

He turned and looked Thomasito in the eye.

"We don't allow that *trash* here. Y*ou are correct,*" Thomasito said, then feigned spitting as though just talking about it required cleansing.

Lasher continued, "Clearly, I am done here. No cover, no reason to hang around. Do you know anything about Panama Red? Can you point me in the right direction?"

"Sorry, *friend*. I wouldn't know where to start with that. Now, beer? We are *best friends* when it comes to *beer*."

"Can you help me out? I just need enough intel on the edges, nothing deep. *Can you ask around for me?*" Lasher said.

Thomasito thought for a moment. "Sure, *my friend*. I've got a *family* here in the neighborhood. It is my home. I'm no friend of the *Narcotraficante*."

Lasher nodded, reached into his pocket, pulled out five American twenty-dollar bills, and handed them to Thomasito, who took them and put them in his pocket. "*Thank you*," he said in Spanish.

Panama used American currency, which made this kind of thing a lot easier.

FRIENDS

L asher had Thomasito and his guys leave after helping him move the two DEA agents from the floor to his couch. They were beaten badly. Some of the hair on the back of their heads had been pulled off by the tape.

Blue Shirt looked like he would be awake in a few minutes. Their wounds were probably not life-threatening, but they were severe wounds, none-theless. If they could maintain their calm, Lasher would drive them to the hospital after he talked with them.

He sat in the oversized chair opposite the couch, waiting. Eventually, Blue Shirt, William Walker, picked his head up, looking around the room con-fused. Then he saw Lasher and focused on him.

Lasher smiled at the man and said, "*We're all friends here, amigo.*"

A confused look crossed Walker's face. He went to shake his head but instantly groaned and put his hand up to the back of his head where Thomasito had clobbered him.

"It's probably a concussion," Lasher said. "I broke your nose too, sorry. I reset it while you were still unconscious, as a friendly gesture"—Lasher opened both arms to suggest the same—"but it's broken in at least one place."

They sat in silence for a few moments, Walker out of it. Then he spoke, "Why didn't you just give us the challenge-response?"

Anger flared in Lasher. "Why did you and your friend try to be tough guys?"

Walker nodded, gingerly touching his nose and wincing at the slightest contact.

"So you know," Lasher said in a friendly enough tone, "my handlers didn't get me the contact information until I called them a few minutes ago while you were out. I had no idea you were coming."

"Damn, army, *fifars*," Walker said, leaning back on the couch.

Lasher got up and went to the kitchen, returning with ice rolled in a dishtowel. "Put this on the back of your neck. Or your nose, whichever hurts worse."

Walker took the wrap, leaning forward, then back, dizzy. He put it on the back of his neck, then realized that Yellow Shirt, Citlai, was still unconscious. He turned to look at him slowly, then leaned back so he could see the back of Citlai's head where he had hit the pavement.

"Christ, is he alright?" he said to Lasher.

"I think so. I need to get both of you to the hospital, but I want to talk to you first." Lasher got up and went back to the window. He liked to look outside; it somehow got his brain going and helped him diffuse the anger.

Walker watched Lasher, then looked back at Citlai, putting his hand on Citlai's neck to check his pulse, looking closely at the head wound.

"I think he needs to go to the hospital now. We can talk on the way."

Lasher nodded, willing to concede. He certainly didn't want to be responsible for the death of a DEA agent, and Walker was acting reasonably.

The two of them carried Citlai to Lasher's car, parked behind the house. It was a fifteen-year-old Toyota sedan, given as part of the undercover assignment. They put Citlai in the back seat, being careful not to allow his head to bump into the doorjamb when they put him in.

Lasher closed the door and got in the driver's seat, Walker in the passenger seat. These were three big men in a big car.

Lasher started the car and drove out of the alley. It was dark out, and this part of the city streets was not well lit. "It's about twenty minutes to the hospital. Tell me what you wanted to meet about."

Walker looked out the window, then at Lasher. There was anger underneath his gaze. Lasher could not tell if it was directed at him or simply Walker being irritated that he handled the situation so poorly.

"We got a lead on where they are growing the cocoa and mixing with the weed to make Panama Red. The word is that there is a big operation in southeastern Panama. We were told you are working informants on the ground. We're supposed to contact you and form a joint task force with the army, so we fall within the treaty to operate near the southern border near Columbia."

Lasher looked at him sideways for a few moments. "Why the tough-guy act?" He wanted to settle that before anything else. It was a dumb move on their part.

If I weren't their contact, had they pulled that stunt with, say, Thomasito, or one of the other gang members, I would be driving their dead bodies to the morgue, not their live ones to the hospital.

"We were told we should establish ourselves as people not to be messed with, as *enforcers*."

Lasher turned his head. "Well, that was some darn bad advice. Most of the people here are not *Narcotraficante.* They hate it as much as you or I. But they are territorial and tough. Your bonehead act would have gotten both of you killed in that neighborhood. They're not *Narcotraficante,* but they are tough *Mafiosos*."

Lasher pushed his anger away. He had been a stupid American, too, initially. Not having learned how things got done here, trying to be a tough guy. But he learned quickly enough. He was lucky that way, and based upon his conversation with Thomasito, given his cover was blown even before he arrived, he was glad he had learned how to take a more diplomatic approach.

"To get along here, you need to be more *amigo* and less *ahuevado,*" Lasher said to Walker. "More friend and less egghead."

Walker nodded his understanding. "Well, then, aren't we lucky we ran into you first," he said, gingerly touching his nose again. Both he and Lasher smiled an ironic smile, but it was too dark in the car now for either to see the other.

SHOPPING

S harp walked down the poorly lit street in a thin, expensive red dress, carrying shopping bags from the high-end outlets. Night had just fallen. Hernando walked just behind her, carrying even more bags with marquee brand names on them.

They had taken the long way home. While Mexico City was massive and vastly dangerous, there were sections, like where Sharp kept her condo, that were generally nice and safe. She could have easily gone straight home from the shopping mall with little chance of any problems.

God doesn't fear mortals; mortals fear God. It's time to remind them.

So, just a few blocks away from the civilized areas, she and Hernando stood out like a blinking red light in the night. It was almost unfair to suggest that bad actors wished them harm in the same way an alligator was a bad actor if it wanted to eat a chicken. More instinct than motivation, what was an alligator going to do, not eat the stupid chicken walking into its mouth?

She could feel the predatory eyes on her as they made their way down the street, picturing them like in a cartoon, big red blinking eyes in the shadows with disembodied tongues licking their lips, not believing their good fortune.

If it seems too good to be true, my dear subordinates: it almost certainly is.

When she felt she had command of a good-sized audience, she dropped a bag and made a big show of bending over to pick it back up, dropping another bag in the process.

Hernando rolled his eyes, knowing this game and what it required of him, always surprised to the degree Sharp committed herself to these charades.

On cue, several men stepped out, suddenly surrounding the two outsiders from nowhere.

A tall, tough-looking man with a scar that ran from his forehead to his cheek seemed to be the leader. "*Hello, ma'am. Good day,*" he said. "*May we assist you with your groceries?*"

Sharp smiled at him. *Always good to know who is in charge.* She looked at Hernando—they exchanged a knowing glance—then back to the man who spoke. When she looked at him, she saw that the eye the scar was over was a milky white.

"*These aren't groceries!*" Oh, she loved playing a stupid character. The anticipation was building. "*These designer clothes cost more than you make in a year! Please step aside.*"

There were four other men, five total. Two stepped closer to Hernando, two closer to Sharp.

The lead man looked hard at Sharp, then even harder at Hernando, sensing something was off. No one was this stupid; he could feel on the edges that he may not be the alligator here.

Sharp saw the look and felt disappointment.

Signaling to step away to his four friends, he said, "*Ma'am. Our mistake. Please enjoy your evening,*" and stepped to the side to offer Sharp the sidewalk.

"*Do it,*" Sharp said to Hernando.

In an instant, the bags were dropped, Hernando striking the man closest with a fist and kicking another man's knee with his foot before the bags hit the ground. A knife flashed from a third man, Hernando quickly disarming him and sticking the freed blade into the man's neck.

He saw that the fourth man ran away.

The leader thought quickly, grabbing Sharp in a chokehold, walking backward, clearly spooked by Hernando. It was a good grip he had, one arm around her throat, the other holding it at the wrist, ready to apply deadly pressure.

Hernando straightened, looking around. He bent

down, removing the knife from its still-spasming victim, standing back up, feeling the blade, moving it in his hands, getting a feel for its balance.

Sharp was beside herself with excitement; this had gone better than she could have hoped. The leader had her tight. He was strong. She could feel the weakness of her neck in its awkward position, feeling the man's strength as he slowly moved her back up the street.

"*Do it,*" she said softly, looking Hernando in the eye.

"*What?*" her assailant said, not understand the comment, becoming unsure.

She ignored him. "*Do it.*" Louder.

Hernando heard her and knew what she wanted. He flipped the knife over several times, blade first, handle first, blade first, handle first.

"*Do It!*" she yelled as a powerful command, using so much force in her cry that she nearly caused the leader to let her go.

Hernando shrugged and threw the knife hard right at her. She froze, thrilled, not willing to flinch or move dare she misread Hernando's accuracy.

As fast as lighting, the blade flew through the air, striking the man holding her in the forehead, penetrating enough to knock him back where he fell. Sharp stood frozen for a second, Hernando bending down to pick up the bags that had been dropped.

"*Leave them,*" Sharp said, the thrill over, losing interest. This wasn't it; it didn't happen. "*Let's go to Tiempo Divertido. I'm hungry.*"

Tiempo Divertido was one of her favorite restaurants. It wasn't too far back in the direction they had come from, albeit in a much nicer part of town.

"There is blood on your dress," Hernando told her, noticing splatter from the man behind her.

"Don't worry." She put a knowing hand on his shoulder, being sincere. "It's not mine."

BALBOA

The hospital admitted both agents; they each had serious concussions. Lasher agreed to come back tomorrow and talk to Walker.

He got in his car and drove back to the house, getting there just after nine o'clock at night. He used a garden hose to rinse the blood off the front walkway. After that, he paced back and forth in the small main room, walking over to the window and looking out every second or third time he went around the room.

He was debating with himself on a next step, still fighting a wave of underlying anger with the two DEA agents for how they handled things. His thoughts traced back to the afternoon events. This was a technique he developed over years of field-work. Revisualize what happened and try to look for things you missed in real-time.

Why hadn't Williams come out with the briefing on the DEA agents? he thought, finally finding the apparent gap. His anger should be with the Army hierarchy. They put him in this situation, not Walker or the DEA.

Sergeant Jack Williams had been Lasher's peer inside army intelligence for a decade. Lasher elected to apply for warrant officer as soon as he was eligible with five years in service. Williams was comfortable riding out his remaining time as a mid-ranking enlisted soldier. They were not friends nor rivals; each was simply around the other due to their military occupational specialty (MOS) and their identical time in service.

It had been several years, yet Williams never entirely accepted Lasher as outranking him. Nothing overt, but a mild constant undercurrent to their frequent interactions. All that said, Williams was no slouch and would have delivered the information to Lasher, all other things being equal.

It was getting close to ten o'clock. Lasher realized there was no way he would get any sleep. His mind was racing; things were getting interesting.

A large majority of the fieldwork he did in Panama was trivial stuff.

When not undercover like now, the job was to perform background checks and interviews for Army personnel whose security clearance needed to be renewed. It was a constant bureaucratic flow of paperwork.

Even the undercover work, like up until this afternoon, was mundane stuff; running low-level informants to gather general information fed back up to INSCOM through their S2 shop. You rarely were given the big picture as a field agent, almost never related to above battalion-level dealings.

He walked to the bedroom and laid out some of his more presentable civilian clothes. A very appreciated side benefit of the job was that he rarely had to wear a uniform. The Army regulations stipulated that special agents were to wear civilian clothes even during normal on-base operations.

He took a shower and washed his hair, shaving his beard off in the shower as well. Easier to do it that way, given its growth, than at the mirror over the sink. The cat scratch was red. He washed it and put a bandage on it.

I should have gotten some antiseptic at the hospital, and I should have cleaned this cut sooner.

Once dressed and more presentable, he holstered his Springfield XDM sidearm and drove to Quarry Heights in Balboa. It was at the front edge of the canal zone and was where the S2 shop was. Not Captain Crostino and Bravo company; they were at Fort Clayton, a few miles farther north along the run of the canal.

The drive was uneventful this late at night. During the day, it would have taken three times as long; heavy traffic, kids at the stop lights with squeegees trying to get a quarter for washing your windshield. Taxi drivers darting in and out of their lanes, street vendors in the middle of the road, slowing everything down.

Even so, it took about thirty minutes to get there. The city got progressively nicer the closer he got to Balboa, moving from dire city slums to more affluent areas, the canal zone, and finally to Quarry Heights. The joint administrative district in the zone was shared by the governments of Panama and the United States.

Quarry Heights had two components: the lower administrative buildings shared by both governments and the secure upper area. The upper site was built into the mountain proper, only accessible from a winding road going high up Ancon Hill, with entry allowed only to US military and government personnel.

The lower buildings were built in a grand style, made from granite, large open structures with square corners and thick pillars up on hills with long walkways and green manicured lawns leading up to them. It was a style all its own. Not entirely military, but not quite colonial either. The buildings did impress. Driving by them at night, they were well lit and regal.

Lasher drove by, the buildings taking his mind, briefly, off replaying the day over and over again in his head. Instead, impressed as always, with the architect's grand design, conveying so much authority through buildings. As a Panamanian citizen, you felt like you were going somewhere special when you visited these structures.

He drove up the hill, the road winding around it several times from bottom to top. It was a slow climb, and Lasher's thoughts went back to replaying the day. He needed to get answers to two questions. First, where was Williams? Why didn't he deliver the information to Lasher when he was supposed to? Second, who was it that ran the undercover ops in the same house and the same way over and over, so much so that it seemed everyone knew that whoever moved in there was a US government agent?

William's location gave him an uneasy feeling in the pit of his stomach, the answer about the house getting him worked up and angry. As a warranted MI field officer, Lasher was used to doing the little jobs. It wasn't flashy work, but it was necessary for the big picture, even if he often dealt with the small elements. Still, suppose the PDF arrested him while he was in civilian clothes spying in their country. In that case, he could spend twenty years in a Panamanian prison, hoping that the latest round of new bureaucrats sent to the embassy found his file and tried to negotiate for his release.

About a third of the way up was the entry gate.

There were six military police (MP) operating the station. Stationary barricades were on either side and a barricade that raised and lowered blocking the road. The automated heavy barrier in the road had been installed a few years ago after a suicide bomber destroyed the US Embassy in Beirut.

Lasher showed his ID. The MP waved him through, the road barricade slowly lowering to let him pass. He drove the rest of the way to the entrance to the tunnels, parked his car in a visitor spot, turned it off, then found himself sitting in the dark and not getting out.

I've got two more months at the house on this assignment, he thought to himself. *No one knows my cover is blown, and no one probably cares.*

Lasher did not get a lot of energy from chasing down low-level pot dealers. He would never touch the stuff, but his mom had found relief in it as she slowly died of cancer, which was why his grandfather raised him. He had not put much thought into it until now, Thomasito's reaction to the Panama Red staying with him.

Panama Red was a different animal altogether.

Sold as expensive pot, it was laced with crack cocaine. The problem was one hit, and some people were hooked for life, unlike regular pot. It could be worse; while you could not overdose on marijuana, you easily could on Panama Red. Thomasito was right to keep it out of his neighborhood.

Lasher decided he would be the right thing to do to end its distribution everywhere. Working with the

DEA presented a unique opportunity he was not usually given.

The US-Panama treaty allowed the US military tremendous latitude in how and where it operated inside Panamanian borders. Signed in 1977, the treaty put in place a US exit strategy, handing the canal zone and canal operations to Panama at the end of 1999. Other US agencies, like the DEA, did not have such latitude as called out in the treaty document. As an easy way around it, the US would attach any agency operatives they wanted in the country to a military unit liaison.

Mostly the military operatives just got out of the way, understanding the loophole being used. However, on paper, if Lasher were going to be the point Army agent for the DEA taking on Panama Red production in the country, he would technically have a lot of flexibility and pull.

That leaves the same two questions, he thought. *Where is Williams, and who keeps sending our agents to get made at the house?*

He had intended to bring himself in but changed his mind, glad he took the time to think things through.

He got out of his car and walked up to the guarded entrance. It was quite the spectacle. Dug into the side of the mountain, a huge metal door like a giant bank vault cracked open, behind four rows of cement barricades, with two MP stations on either side.

He approached the MPs watching him, showing his investigator's badge instead of his military ID. The badge opened a lot more doors. The MP wrote down his name and badge number, making a note of the time, waving him through.

Inside there was a long hallway that led down a gentle slope, then another entry station. This one had thick bulletproof glass with an MP behind the counter on the other side next to another large, solid metal door. A small metal drawer was pushed out from the counter.

The MI badge that Lasher carried was the same one that the FBI used domestically. It was a soft leather case that looked like a wallet. When opened, it had his badge in the bottom section and a federal ID card in the top area identifying him as a special agent.

Lasher put the MI badge in the drawer along with his sidearm. The guard behind the glass withdrew the drawer and looked at the badge, then to Lasher. He made some more notes on a log, checked the safety, and put the handgun on a shelf with the number four under it, pointing to Lasher, who nodded that he saw the number.

Lasher asked the guard, "Who is the S2 OOW tonight?" OOW was the acronym for *officer on watch.* Each command, at every level, always had an OOW and a CQ. The CQ was usually an enlisted noncommissioned officer "in charge of quarters." Basically, around to make sure nothing suddenly burst into flames and log people in and out of the building.

The MP looked at Lasher for a moment, sizing him up, then apparently finding no concerns, said, "Lieutenant Gleason."

Nope. No good. Raced through Lasher's mind.

Gleason was a new second lieutenant. He wouldn't know anything and most likely wouldn't be able to look anything up.

Lasher shook his head at the MP. "Nope. Who's the general's driver tonight?"

The MP smirked to himself, probably reaching the same conclusion about Gleason that Lasher did. He rolled his chair over to another clipboard on the wall, flipped some pages, then rolled back.

"Specialist Mariana," the MP said.

Lasher knew her; this was good luck. She was in Charlie company, the intelligence analysts.

This was excellent luck. An enlisted MOS 97G had access to all the computer systems and files. The 97G was the intelligence analyst. They pieced together all of the field agent reports, including Lashers. They pulled actual intel out of them and into summaries for the upper brass or whoever it was that actually read this stuff.

Further, he knew Sarah Mariana on a more personal level. She was a *Puertorriqueños*, a Puerto Rican. When she first arrived, Lasher was CQ that night. Another soldier traveling with her was pretty drunk when he arrived and had apparently decided that the two were a couple. She confidentially asked Lasher for help, and he cleared the matter up quickly, putting the fear of God into her traveling companion.

The assignment as the general's driver was another rotating duty.

Most MI enlisted at the company level would pull the duty at least once in their sixteen-month in-country tour. Interestingly, you never actually drove the general anywhere. Instead, you were on call to drive the very nice executive sedan to pick up dignitaries, drop off dignitaries, or do other odd tasks as assigned.

The duty was for seventy-two hours at a time.

It was a sweet deal. The duty position was in a nice room in the mountain with a couch for sleeping, a TV, and a refrigerator that was well stocked. You were actually encouraged to sleep as much as you could since the driving assignments could come at any moment. Mostly they didn't; how many dignitaries arrived in Panama at eleven at night?

Heck, how many arrived at all?

In your seventy-two-hour shift, you would be in the minority if you got told to go anywhere. And the icing on the cake is you got three days off after pulling the duty to recover since technically you could have been busy the whole time. If the shift rolled between weekends, you could end up with a nine-day paid vacation.

Lasher took his badge back out of the metal drawer and nodded to the MP, who hit a button somewhere, making a buzzing noise. Lasher pushed the door next to the MP station, heard it unlatch, and started to walk down another long hallway.

RESEARCH

L asher was sitting at the small kitchen-like table in the driver's ready room. Mariana was on the computer typing in search terms. She was good on the computer, growing up near Washington, D.C., to two parents who had government careers. They made sure she had access to computers and that she received a good education. Mariana's mother was the deputy director for the Defense Intelligence Agency (DIA). She kept to herself, not wanting preferential treatment because of it.

Most of the MI information was stored in separate files in the system, purposely fragmented and with low levels of availability. However, current agent assignments were in a roster that many could access.

The assignments were just a list of agent call signs and project code names. Lasher's current job was on Project Raincloud. The project words and call signs didn't mean anything by themselves; you had to know the active projects, a separate list.

Fortunately, Lasher did know the different codes. The roster said that Williams was on Project Gumball and had just been assigned to it a week ago. He was probably supposed to stop by and give Lasher the information about the DEA agents on his way to Gumball.

Project Gumball was another low-level investigation focused on collecting information about the new banking infrastructure being built out in the financial district. It was suspected that local contractors were skimming off local materials. A good percentage of the computer hardware kept going missing. They were looking for intel on what they thought was a local criminal enterprise moving the computer hardware in a local underground market.

"Can you access any specific project files?" Lasher asked Mariana.

She turned back to him. "You mean like Project Gumball? No, not unless I am assigned as the analyst for it, which I am not."

"I was thinking more about Project Raincloud. Actually, I want to know what project was run out of the house I am in for Raincloud. And if there was a project before that running from the same house."

Mariana thought for a moment. "I don't think there is any index like that in the system, at least not at our level."

They both sat there in silence. Then Lasher had a thought. "What about motor pool records? Can you access those?"

She had a quizzical look across her face, most likely wondering how the change in focus fits with the earlier information. But she did have access to the motor pool records; they were not classified.

"Yes, for our battalion anyway. You have access also; I think everyone with a system ID has access."

Lasher stood up. "Okay, tell you what. Log out and let me log in; that way, it's not the same ID querying both files."

Mariana logged out, stood up, and walked back over to the couch, where she had been sitting watching TV when Lasher had entered. "Do you need any help in the field with analysis?" she asked Lasher hopefully. The 97Gs always wanted to do fieldwork; they saw the civilian clothes and the badges and wanted in on the deal.

Lasher smiled. "How much longer are you the driver?"

"I just came on yesterday, so I'm about halfway through. A little over a day left." She was just the slightest bit hopeful.

"Okay, we'll see. I might need help depending on how the next twenty-four hours go. Write down the authorization for your dispatch. If I need you, I will call it in."

Each driver was given a word or short phrase that was specific just for their shift. Since the phone could ring and the drivers did not always know everyone who was allowed to assign them, they only acted on orders over the phone line that included their authorization code.

Mariana was, of course, not supposed to give it out, but it was okay because Lasher was not authorized to use it. Perfect military symmetry.

Lasher logged in with his credentials. "How do I access the motor pool records?" he asked Mariana.

She came over, leaning over his shoulder and pressing a few number keys, navigating the system menu. She was leaning in closer than she needed to. Lasher was glad he had showered, not minding the harmless flirting.

"It's right here in the battalion menu," she said, standing up after getting the computer through the menus to the vehicle records.

"I need to search by VIN and see who else has been assigned the car I have," Lasher said, looking back.

He was half hoping she would lean in again, but instead, she walked back to the couch, already bored with him, and said, "Hit the function key and the number two. That brings up the search. Its name-value pairs, so type in Victor India November (VIN), a comma, and then the VIN you want to get the records for."

He put the information in and the check-in/out records for the car displayed on the screen.

"Let me have that paper you wrote the authorization on." He leaned back.

She handed it to him, along with the pen.

Sure enough, the car got checked out about every seven months for ninety days, then returned.

It had been going on for the past four years. He wrote down the dates and the names of the people who had been assigned the car. He folded the paper and put it in his pants pocket, thanked Mariana, and walked back out to his car, checking out at each MP station just as he had on the way in, retrieving his Springfield XDM 9MM on the way out of the tunnel.

CRUZ

I t was just past midnight; Lasher couldn't get Williams not delivering the message to him out of his head. The field check-ins were weekly, so if Williams headed out two days ago, there were still five days before he would be missed. Lasher considered working through channels, but he knew that would go nowhere.

He started the car and drove to Fort Clayton, the main Army post back down the mountain, being checked out the same as he was checked in.

The MPs at the gate to Fort Clayton went through their own routine of checking his ID then waved him on.

The base did not have as many barricades and checkpoints as Quarry Heights, but it had enough. He drove past the main administrative buildings near the front of the base. They were massive three-story brick buildings in a horseshoe shape, surrounding a grassy field used for military parades and morning exercise. The area was a hundred yards across and two hundred yards long.

Fort Clayton was built up from lowlands with the fill from digging the Panama Canal early in the century. It sat directly adjacent to one of the largest of the twelve locks along the run of the canal. Lasher knew the base well. He drove slowly; the base speed limit was eighteen miles per hour, an odd speed, but strictly enforced by patrolling MPs even this late at night.

Leaving the administrative section of the base, he drove past hundreds of villas.

These were the small, well-built houses for military families. Everything on Clayton was built with concrete blocks and reinforced, even the family homes. Concern for everything from hurricanes to a possible canal breach made it crucial for even the housing to be as sturdy as possible. Eventually, he saw the road he was looking for and turned left, heading into one of a hundred identical nondescript housing areas.

He pulled up to number 404 on Croft Street, turned the car off, got out, and knocked on the ornate metal door. He knocked loud enough to be heard but tried to keep it as unobtrusive as possible.

After his second set of knocks, he saw lights come on, and after a few moments, Warrant Officer Jim Cruz opened the door angrily. He was wearing his PT (physical training) clothes. Many soldiers did this; they slept in the shirt and shorts they would need to be in for morning exercises. It saved them ninety seconds of getting dressed, which was ninety seconds more sleep every day.

When Cruz saw it was Lasher, his demeanor changed. Cruz was a W1, a first-grade warrant officer; Lasher was a W3. As a W3, Lasher was considered a field grade officer, the same as a major in entitlements and respect, but technically outranked by the lowliest of second lieutenants on their first day of commission.

The US Army, and most militaries, had four types of soldier ranks. The first were privates; this was a soldier in their most basic conception and the lowest ranking of all soldiers. Privates were enlisted; they signed a contract that stipulated their service in exchange for pay over a duration. After three or four years, a private could become a noncommissioned officer (NCO), basically a sergeant. There existed a myriad of types of sergeants, each denoting a step on the career ladder.

Then there were the commissioned officers. Junior grade like lieutenants and captains (also sometimes called company grade), then field grade (major through colonel), and then general grade (generals had almost as many career-ladder steps as sergeants).

Nestled in the middle was the platypus, something called a warrant officer. All warrant officers had first enlisted and made the rank of sergeant. After five years and no longer than eight years after enlistment, a sergeant could petition to become a warrant officer, proclaiming highly specialized skills in a particular area. If selected and after stock training programs, they could become "warranted" to operate as a highly-skilled, single-track specialist.

Warrant officers outranked all enlisted personnel and were outranked by all traditional commissioned officers.

But the military couldn't keep it that simple.

A grade one warrant officer was considered still enlisted in terms of seniority. They were an enlisted noncommissioned officer with a warrant to act as a specialist.

A chief warrant officer grade two received a commission, moving from the ranks of the noncommissioned officers to the commissioned.

A chief warrant officer of grade three was commissioned and categorized as a field grade officer, placing them conceptually but not specifically in a higher privilege class than company-level officers like captains, even though they did not outrank them, and even often reported to a captain at the company level.

The only essential thing about all this was that Lasher got paid the same as a major, and if he wanted it, he got better housing.

Not that Cruz's house here was all that bad.

"Who is it?" a female voice from inside the home called to Cruz. Lasher knew Cruz was waiting for his family to arrive, so he was living in a house and not in the barracks. Lasher also knew they were not here yet, so whoever was calling out was not Cruz's wife.

Cruz called back *"Nobody,"* in Portuguese, then walked out and closed the front door. He and Lasher now stood on the front porch.

"What is it, Chief?" Cruz said once the door was fully closed.

"You were working Gumball up until a couple of days ago?" Lasher asked.

"I'm still working on it, but yes, I was in the field for the past couple of months on it," Cruz said. It came out more like a question.

"Did you brief Williams before he went out?"

"Sure, we spent the last week transitioning. Why?"

"Williams was supposed to stop by my place two days ago with important information, but he didn't. I need to find him and ask him why." It came out simple and accurate, but Lasher feared the situation was getting more complicated by the minute.

"You want me to give you the address of the house we are using?" Cruz asked. "It is a condo, pretty nice." He turned to look back at the house like he wanted to get back to bed.

"No. Get dressed; you're coming with me," Lasher said.

A look of determination crossed Cruz's face. He was digging into that part of a soldier's brain to follow orders when they didn't want to.

Lasher continued, seeing the expression. "Do you have a sidearm here? A handgun or something?"

"I have my personal M9," Cruz said.

"Get dressed and bring it. We need to move now while we have time." Lasher walked back to the car and started it, waiting for Cruz. After a few minutes, Cruz came out dressed as roughly as Lasher was in blue jeans and a T-shirt. Cruz's shirt said: *Coca-Cola, it's the real thing.*

Lasher briefly wondered what that could possibly mean. Coke wasn't the real thing anymore; it hadn't been since early in the century when they took the cocaine out of it. As an army special agent, one of the running jokes was that you should always "deny everything and make loud counteraccusations" in an interview.

Coke seemed desperate in the same way; claim you are what you used to be.

Fake it 'til you make it; Lasher remembered wisdom from his grandfather.

Cruz got in the passenger's seat, his M9 in a holster that put the weapon to his left side; the bulge was apparent under his T-shirt.

Lasher backed the car out and started driving to exit the base. "Tell me what you told Williams."

Cruz looked over to Lasher. "Can we stop at the mess hall and get some coffee to go?"

There was a twenty-four-hour mess in the administrative building near the front gate. Lasher pulled the car up to a waiting area. Cruz spent about five minutes inside, then emerged with two cups of coffee in medium-sized white styrofoam cups with black plastic lids.

The drive would take about thirty minutes at this time of night, turning left out of Clayton onto Av Omar Torrijos Herrera. The Av Omar was named after some Panamanian military officer from the 1960s. It ran the length of the canal and then along the Bay of Panama. You just basically stayed on this road—it eventually transitioned to the Interamericana Highway—then it would dump you into Marbella, their destination.

Marbella was one of the nicer parts of the city, where a lot of the newer high-rises were built. There were a lot of embassies in the area too.

As they made the left, exiting Fort Clayton, Cruz began talking. "They are building a new world banking center in Marbella. Very modern stuff. They ran fiber optic cable to it last year. High-speed computer connections. It's all being funded by the Global Bank Group, GBG. They made some deals with Noriega to expand the already significant financial market presence here in Panama.

"There are two core contractors: some group of Swedes they flew in, and a company called *Suministros de Construcción,* which is owned by Noriega by way of at least two different shell companies."

Cruz paused to take a drink of his coffee, then continued. "All that is well and good, and as you know, we are not the building police. A lot of the construction work has been started. What we're investigating is the computer equipment itself. A good deal of it keeps going missing.

"No one is even supposed to have access to it while in storage. They're worried about the Russians bugging it. How they would do that is beyond me, but our investigation is simple. We've been working to find out if there is a black market or some transportation system that is selling, then moving out of the country, all this expensive computer stuff.

"It looks more likely that the equipment is being moved out of the country than coming back to be sold here in Panama. We've found dockworkers working late at night and then not showing up for their regular shift the next day, suddenly not needing the money. Stuff like that.

"There is also the PDF substation that has a large warehouse attached to it. I got as far as suspecting that the computer equipment would get moved from the construction site to the PDF warehouse, then put on boats by the dockworkers, and off it goes. I am still working on where it goes.

"Williams was to pick that up and provide surveillance on the dock, see if we can get some vessel registration IDs or even just see what flag they are flying."

Cruz drank some of his coffee again.

Lasher was listening intently. "Where should Williams be right now, given how you were running things when you were there?"

Cruz thought for a moment. "It would depend. If he got a tip that something was being moved, he could be at the dock. If not, he should be asleep in the condo we're using."

"Let's try the condo first," Lasher said.

ELEVATOR

The condo was in a mid-level high-rise nestled between the highway and the Bay of Panama. It was an older building, not part of the new economic boom of building that Panama was enjoying. It was made of cement block with paint chipping here and there. The condo unit was on the ninth floor. Just too many stories to want to take the stairs. The elevator had two security doors, a new external metal door, and the original internal security door. They both opened with the same key.

Cruz opened the doors and pushed the UP button. The internal automatic elevator door immediately opened, the elevator already on the bottom floor. Lasher walked past Cruz and got in, Cruz fiddling with the external doorway, then relocked both. Cruz put the key in a slot by the floor numbers and pressed nine.

The pulley system creaked and moaned as it lifted the elevator. The ride up was a little unnerving, not smooth at all, the elevator proper grinding against something metal on metal. The door opened on the ninth floor, and they both got off. Only the first floor had an extra door to the elevator. Cruz led the way down the hall; there were only six units on each floor, three on each side. He stopped at a middle door on the right and opened it with the same key.

The place had been turned upside down. There wasn't a lot in the one-bedroom unit to start with. No personal items. A table and chairs. A couch and TV. Some basic pots and pans, cleaning supplies, a couple sets of sheets, and towels.

What there was had been thrown into the middle of the room. All the cupboards were open, all the drawers pulled out and on the floor. Lasher couldn't tell if there were a struggle, just a frantic search, or both.

Cruz was stunned. "What the hell happened? I was just here three days ago. I stayed here for a couple months."

The elevator made the sound of doors closing and going back down to the first floor. The condo door was open; the soft screeching of metal on metal came in from the hallway. Lasher ran out to the hall and watched the floor indicators. The elevator went down to the first floor, then almost immediately started heading back up.

Lasher drew his sidearm and signaled to Cruz to do

the same. He quickly looked up and down the hall. There was no leverage point; it was just a straight hallway with the elevator on one end, three doors on each side, the hallway maybe fifty feet.

Cruz looked at Lasher for instructions, his M9 drawn and his eyes wide. Lasher stayed in the door frame, looking down at the elevator. He made a fist in the air, telling Cruz to hold steady and wait. Cruz leaned against the opposite wall inside the condo and crouched down with the M9 at the ready.

The elevator kept climbing; six, seven, eight. Lasher tightened his grip on his XDM, extending his arm straight down, ready to raise it if he needed to.

Nine. Nothing happened. Ten. Eleven.

It stopped at twelve.

Lasher relaxed, causing Cruz to relax. Lasher put his index finger in the air and spun it in a circle. "Check everything really quick. I'm gonna stay here at the door." Cruz scanned the condo, going from room to room. There was nothing but the mess, no other clues. He returned to Lasher, still at the ready in the door, watching the elevator not move.

"There is nothing here," Cruz spoke very softly. "None of Williams's stuff is here either. He would have had a duffle bag with at least a week's worth of civilian clothes, a shaving kit, a book to read."

Lasher put his XDM away. "It's in the air. Do you feel it?"

Cruz holstered his M9. "Yep. They got him. Shit."

Lasher made a face.

"Sorry, nucking futs, shoot," Cruz corrected.

Most soldiers swore profusely, but you stopped doing it around Lasher pretty quickly. Even top brass would eventually stop swearing around Lasher. It was like he had some supernatural ability to make you feel uncomfortable about it.

Cruz had asked him a hundred times already why; Lasher always just told him that he didn't like it. It wasn't really an answer, but it always made sense in the moment.

They closed the door and headed to the stairs to go down, not risking the elevator.

On the way down in the stairwell, Lasher said, "Isn't there a PDF substation near here?"

Cruz nodded that there was.

"If they took him, they took him there," Lasher said, using one hand on the handrail as they descended. "How long before they move him to *Cárcel Modelo*, or worse?"

The "Modern Prison" had been used for years. It was best described as a graveyard for the living. A prison run by the PDF in the worst possible way. Guards, thugs. Little food. No clean water. Dysentery, beatings. Once Williams was in there, it would take a miracle to get him out.

Lasher handed Cruz the car keys. "You drive. Take me to the substation."

Cruz took the keys, a look of curiosity on his face. "What's the plan, Chief? We can't just go knock on the PDF door and ask to see Williams."

Lasher looked at him, a determined look in his eye. "That's exactly what I am going to do."

Cruz got in the driver's seat but didn't start the car. "We need to report this to Crostino. She can bring in the big guns."

Lasher sat in the passenger seat with the door open, the interior car light on. He unholstered his XDM, checking the load. "Jim, you know that the US won't admit we're out here. You signed the waiver just like I did. If we're captured, we're on our own. Williams will spend the rest of his short life in a Panamanian jail.

"We get him back now before he's moved. It's the only way."

Cruz looked at Lasher for a bit, then nodded and started the car.

WILLIAMS

The PDF substation was a flat one-story building down a side street with a large parking lot. There were six PDF patrol cars parked in the lot, and a larger Light Armored Vehicle (LAV) with an M60 gun mount on the top and three large tires on either side.

The front of the substation faced the parking lot. The double doors were clear plate glass. Lasher had been in similar buildings; they were not heavily fortified. There would be an entry area, a few offices, a large locker room for the officers to change and shower, and a few holding cells.

Cruz pulled the car up right in front of the doors at precisely 2 a.m.

Lasher opened his door, and the interior light came on. His face was serious. "Keep it running," was all he said to Cruz. He got out and walked with authority down the short walkway and through the doors.

There was a young officer at the desk. He was half asleep, his eyes opening wider when he saw Lasher enter.

Lasher quickly looked around. There was no one else visible in the building. He stopped at the desk, opened the sign-in book, and wrote *Daffy Duck, 2 AM* in nearly legible script with the pen attached by a metal chain.

Then looking authoritatively at the desk officer who was watching Lasher, not fully understanding, he said, "*I'm here for the American. Williams.*" He spoke in Castilian Spanish with perfect upper-class inflections. He could have sounded like a schoolteacher to the young officer. His tone was as if he were ordering a brand-new private in basic training.

The officer turned to look to the back of the building.

Good, Lasher thought. *I think Williams is still here. It's a natural thing to look if he is.*

The desk officer looked from the back of the building to the signature in the book, having no idea what it said, and looked back up to Lasher. "*The captain will be back in the morning at ten,*" he said.

Lasher just stood there as though the man had not spoken.

"*Who are you?*" the desk officer asked after a moment. He was confused. It would not be unusual for something to be going on that he had not been told about, and the man in front of him sounded legit.

Lasher looked annoyed like he was tired of explaining himself. "*Williams is being turned over to us. Your captain sent me; they just made a deal with the embassy.*" He flashed his badge and credentials.

The American government had pull in Panama. While there were growing hostilities between the two entities, a request from an authoritative American with an official-looking badge at 2 a.m. was a very possible legitimate encounter.

The desk officer's name tag said *Sanchez*.

Lasher continued. "*I am supposed to contact an officer Sanchez here at this station. Did they not inform you?*"

As another look crossed his face, Sanchez nodded and got up, walking to the back area. It was through an unlocked metal door. Not quite military-grade but sturdy enough.

He was gone for a few minutes, then returned with two other officers and the look of having just been chewed out. One officer was younger like Sanchez; the other older, probably the watch commander, who was supposed to be awake and working but sleeping in the back, letting the lower-ranking Sanchez do the grunt work of watching the front desk.

"What's this about?" the older man said in English.

Lasher studied him. He was big and gruff. There would be no confusing him into releasing Williams. There had been a real shot with the kid.

Lasher had a flash memory from his teens after getting caught in a lie by his grandfather. *Son*, Grandpa Lasher had told him, *I'm not mad you stole the money; I'm mad you got caught doing it.*

Lasher knew it wasn't good advice even at the time, but he did take a lesson from it. If you get caught, don't admit anything.

The military had a similar theory: *If you took another soldier's gear in place of your own and got away with it, it was a tactical acquisition. If you got caught doing it, it was theft.*

Lasher looked the big man in the eye, doubling down. "*I need to at least talk to Williams if you can't release him until the captain gets in later. Please bring him out here.*" Lasher stayed in a perfect Spanish dialect just in case.

The watch commander thought for a moment, but Lasher could see he was not buying it.

"Of course, my friend." The big man smiled in what was supposed to be a friendly smile, still speaking English. "Why don't you come to the back. I can let you talk to him in his cell."

The alarm bells were ringing in Lasher's head. He knew what was going to happen. They would lock him in the back. The big metal door had a lock on it. If captured, his life would be all but forfeited.

The two men from the back were still slowly advancing. The younger one moved off to the side. Lasher could see he would try and get behind him, around the other side of the desk.

While there was still time, Lasher tried one last feint. *"This is highly irregular. I will come back when your captain is here so we can do this properly."* He started to turn to leave, and the three made their move.

The young officer from the back produced a sap, an illegal but effective weapon, basically a "sock-with-a-rock" in it, only the sock was woven polypropylene, a thick, dense fabric. These weapons were carried by most PDF. Lasher didn't know if they were standard issue or a welcome gift from your fellow officers. Either way, the weapon was high quality and professional. They were also debilitating and near-deadly if used on the head.

Anger flared in Lasher; the stupid kid was swinging the sap for his head. That could kill him. Before he had time to think, his reflexes took over. Years of training in *Kenpo* combined with years of field-work.

The attack came in part from behind him. He turned, moving with the momentum of the kid's swing, grabbing the sap at its base, pulling it out of the kid's grip, and pushing his attacker forward with his already substantial momentum. Lasher continued the move, turning quickly in the swing, bringing the sap down around to whack the kid in the back between the shoulder blades, hard.

He could have easily struck the head, but that would have been fatal. The incredible momentum from the sock-with-a-rock was enough, impacting between the shoulder blades with a loud double crack. The first was the impact from the sap, the second the impact of the officer with the ground.

Lasher continued the spin, landing facing the two remaining men in the room, the sap held in his right hand, the end with the rock caught in his left, ready for another swing. The whole move took only a second, one fluid motion starting with the attacker and ending with Lasher in control.

There was a long moment where nothing happened, time frozen. The PDF officers trying to register what they had just seen, Lasher paused and waited to see their reaction.

The watch commander reacted first, sprinting for the door he had come through and yelling something to someone on the other side.

I can't let him get to the door and lock it! The thought flashed through Lasher's mind. He would never make the distance, so instinctively, he threw the sap as hard and fast as he could. It impacted with a loud thud on the metal door as it closed. *Not good.*

Sanchez, the desk officer, was back behind the

counter, standing, staring at Lasher with a look of panic on his face. Not knowing what else to do with him, Lasher grabbed the front of his uniform with his left hand and swung his now-empty right hand around, grabbing the back of his head and slamming his face down onto the desk. Sanchez slid off the desk onto the ground, knocked out.

Cruz burst into the lobby through the front doors. "No, no, no, no, no!" He was yelling at Lasher as he came in, his weapon drawn. "This is *crazy*! We can't get into a *fight* in a PDF station!"

Lasher jumped over the front desk, motioning for Cruz to advance on the metal door with him, acting quickly while they had time. He drew his XDM from his rear waist with his right hand, undoing a snap with his left hand that held the sidearm in place.

He flipped the safety from black to red, bringing the gun up to a ready position, keeping his elbows in.

For some reason, every recruit that ever existed, when first handed a pistol or rifle and tasked to fire it, stuck their elbows out as far as they could, creating a wider target for an adversary. Lasher learned not to do this when he was very young, going shooting with Grandpa, getting his arms and elbows whacked with a stick. *Do you really want to make it that easy for the Krauts?* His grandpa would ask.

When Lasher got to the door, it was locked. He pulled on the handle a few times with his back against the wall off to the side. Cruz arrived and put his back against the wall on the other side of the door near the hinges.

Cruz let out a string of curses in Spanish. Lasher looked at him, and Cruz said exasperatedly, "Shoot, darn, shucks," with a look of actual irritation on his face.

Lasher made a hand signal telling Cruz to move to the wall behind him on the same side of the door, making a show of aiming his XDM at the door lock. Cruz moved, back to cursing under his breath and shaking his head no.

Lasher stepped away from the door, held up three fingers, then two, then a pause.

The Springfield 9MM rang out loud, breaking the silence that had contained only the internal sound of his heart beating.

Bam bam bam!

Three quick shots, clearing both the door lock and latch.

Lasher pushed himself back up against the side wall and pulled the door open, getting his arm back out of the way as fast as he could.

Someone opened fire from the interior with a semi-automatic rifle, probably an A60 given its five-round burst instead of three. The standard issue for the PDF rifle was the good old AK47. However, hundreds of A60s were also in use, a failed Russian prototype for the heavier AK74 replacement.

One-two-three-four-five! One-two-three-four-five!

The five-pack bursts shot out fast, blowing holes in the door and hitting the back of the desk up front by the entryway.

It wasn't in him to fire blind into a hallway, so Lasher popped his head around the doorframe and back as fast as he could. As soon as he got his head back around, another five-pack rang out, hitting the doorframe near his head, fragmenting some of the drywall, and tearing his shirt sleeve. A metal sound rang out too, the rounds impacting the internal metal door bracing, keeping Lasher from being shot through the wall his back was against.

The cell block was not that long, maybe thirty feet. It was straight, with cells surrounded by metal bars on either side. There were two people down the hall: the watch commander with the machine gun and someone else. The second man had been fumbling with keys when Lasher looked.

If they get into the cells, this will be impossible, Lasher thought. There was no choice.

Another five-pack rang out, then the start of another *one-two-three—click, click.* He would have to reload now. The shots hit about the same spot as before, sending out drywall and tiny metal shards.

Lasher whipped his head away, but the pieces ripped into his arm and side again, one hitting him in the forehead and another in the neck. It was a flesh wound; it didn't even hurt, but blood started to flow out, one stream running down his left cheek and the other down his left forearm.

He moved fast as soon as the last burst stopped, rolling in low, hopefully from an unexpected angle. He opened up with the XDM, shooting in controlled but precise bursts, firing three shots, hitting each man once and the back wall once. When he came out of his roll, he fired again.

Bam bam bam! Pause. *Bam bam bam!*

The noise was so loud with the metal bars and confined area.

Both PDF soldiers were down, hit in the face twice each, the wall behind them a mess.

Cruz slammed through the door behind Lasher. Time froze again. Nothing happened for a beat, then another.

Lasher stayed crouched in his ready position, XDM still aimed down the hall. After a third beat, he motioned for Cruz to move down the hall and secure the area.

Cruz did, moving carefully from cell to cell, making sure there were no more PDF in the area. In the last cell was Williams, laying on the floor. There was no cot in the small space. Williams was beaten badly, big black-and-blue bags under his left eye, blood caked in his hair and running out of his ears. His face was puffy and bloody. He had his arms over his head, protecting it and covering his ears.

"Jack," Cruz whispered as loud as he could.

"Jack!" he had to yell, everyone's ears still ringing from all the small arms fire. Williams looked up. It was slower than it should have been; he wasn't right.

Lasher yelled down the hall, "Get the keys from the guard and get Williams! We have to get out of here *now!*"

PENTHOUSE

S harp was sound asleep when the knock on her door came. She didn't sleep well, or often, so she was exceedingly angry when she was awakened; it was so rare to have moments of restful slumber. There was a second knock, infuriating her even more. She sat up. It was pointless now, raising the purple sleep mask from over her eyes.

Her bedroom was fully lit. She was afraid of the dark, so she always had lights on. The sleeping eye cover did its job well enough. The penthouse master suite was large and luxurious. Her bed was high off the ground on a mattress of extreme quality. Her sheets were Egyptian cotton, her pillows' feathers of the most expensive kind. She enjoyed the feeling of luxury against her nude form.

Sometimes when she could not sleep, she marveled at the pillows.

Were the geese they pulled the feather from alive when they did it? Was it like a crop, pulling the feathers off the live bird then putting them back in cages until they grew feathers back, only to be harvested again?

How fantastic a job that would be, hundreds of birds kept alive just to be tortured, to make pillows. I wonder if there is a public company I could buy that farms feathers?

The other option intrigued her just as much, some nights being able to drift to sleep contemplating the origin of her pillows that her head rested on, feathers pulled from the dead decapitated bodies of giant geese.

Maybe they see the same thing that people do right before they become my pillow? If I keep my head on it, perhaps the visions will come to me when I finally sleep.

There was a third knock. She had drifted off again.

"What!" she called out, allowing her irritation to show, ripping the covers away, walking over to a small table, getting a cigarette. Sharp knew she had a pleasant form. She exercised and ate properly. She was proud of the deep scars lining her back and the cigarette burns on her upper arms and chest. Few could have endured what she had or been willing to pay the price for her current status in life.

The marks were a badge of honor, demonstrating her resolve.

Hernando opened the door and entered the room,

not surprised or interested by her lack of covering. "Ma'am, I am sorry to wake you, but I just received a phone call from one of our liaisons in Panama. The details are a little unclear, but it seems several US soldiers raided the PDF station where we were interrogating the US agent."

Sharp lit her cigarette and threw the lighter at the table. She was irritated but knew that she didn't need theatrics with Hernando. He already understood and was fully committed to the effort.

"And?" she said, wanting to get on with it.

"And," Hernando continued, "they killed the PDF officers and rescued the American."

She flicked her lit cigarette at him. He allowed it to bounce off his shirt, putting it out with his foot when it was on the expensive Mediterranean tile.

"Do we still have that agent's family? The other one, Mister Helpful?" she asked, taking out another cigarette and lighting it.

Hernando made a "kind of" motion with his head and shoulders.

"Really?" Sharp said. "Did you stop feeding them or something?"

Hernando made the same motion again.

They had kidnapped the family of one of the American agents to use as leverage over a month ago. Hernando had gotten bored driving over to the warehouse, so he had left them tied up for over two weeks with no food or water. They eventually just expired.

Sharp put her second cigarette out in the ashtray on the table. She had lit two but had not smoked any. "Well, he doesn't know that. Go ahead and fully activate him. It's now or never."

Hernando nodded and left the room, closing the door behind himself.

Sharp watched him leave.

Now I'm awake. I'm not getting back to sleep for a while, she thought, walking over to a stationary exercise bike. *It's going to be a long night*, she thought to herself as she started pedaling, making a note to call in the morning to see if there were any pillow companies for sale anywhere.

FAMILIA

They got Williams back to Lasher's neighborhood around 3:30 a.m., but they couldn't get to the house. There were several PDF patrol cars in front with their red and yellow lights flashing, and one in the back alley with no lights at all. Lasher saw the lights in time and had Cruz take an alternate route, ending up in the alley behind Tomas's house. Far enough away from the commotion to not be noticed.

People from the neighborhood were out and about, standing in their nightclothes in the road, keeping a reasonable distance, but watching the PDF nonetheless. Several of the gang members were around also, on the edges of things. They would be deciding if the PDF was going to be allowed to leave the neighborhood. The fact they were at the gringo agent's house and not one of theirs probably favored letting the PDF out.

Two guys Lasher recognized saw them in the car in the alley. They walked aggressively over to the car, one with a short club, the other with his right hand behind his back, presumably holding a handgun. Lasher cracked his door, so the car interior light came on, and waved to the two men, then closed the door, so the light went off.

Their stride relaxed, both went around to Lasher's open window.

"*Hoss, they're looking for you,*" the taller one with the hand club said, leaning in and looking at Cruz and Williams. "*What the heck happened? You are a bloody mess. What's wrong with the dude in the back?*" He was indicating Williams. Lasher had been around long enough that even the Panamanian gangs stopped swearing around him.

"*It's bad news all day,*" Lasher said quickly, speaking casually to them as they spoke. "*Is Tomas home? We need a place to hole up.*"

"*It's the revolution all over again,*" the tall man answered, still leaning into the window. "*Thomasito is freaking out. Columbian thugs grabbed his kid and old lady. We were figuring out what to do when these ass—*" He paused. "*When these stupid PDF stormed into your place right up the street.*"

Lasher thought for a few moments, looking at the man in the window, then at Cruz, Williams, then back to the window. "*We'll help Tomas with the Columbians if he'll let us hole up and give my man here*"—he indicated Williams in the back—"*a place to recover. The PDF had him and beat him silly. We just hit their station near Marbella about half an hour ago.*"

The tall man looked at Thomasito's house, then back at Lasher. "*These PDF clowns have been here for the past couple hours, hoss.*" He paused to let that sink in. They were at the house before Lasher left Quarry Heights. "*Let me check with Thomasito.*" Standing back up, he walked to the house.

The man with the gun was not as friendly. He wasn't standoffish either. He was simply there, a few yards back from the car window, waiting for his taller friend to return.

While they all waited, Lasher asked Cruz, "When does your family get here?"

Cruz kept looking out the front of the car. "I waved them off, told them it wasn't safe, too risky to move the whole family here."

Lasher nodded, then thought. "How do you still have the villa?"

Cruz smiled a sheepish smile. "Well…" He was balancing the fact that Lasher was a field grade officer with the truth.

Lasher interrupted to move things along. "Okay, I got it. No one will hear it from me; I don't manage the base housing inventory."

They waited a little while longer. The tall man returned, walking to the window on Lasher's side. "*He said he would have let you hole up here even if you didn't offer to help with the Columbians, but he accepted your offer.*"

It was about 4:00 a.m. by the time Williams was under some blankets on a nice sofa in a room near the back door. Thomasito's two sisters were looking after him. They were both in their late teens and seemed to know how to help someone recover from a beating.

Lasher, Cruz, Thomasito, the tall man whose name turned out to be Alvarez, and three other big guys were all sitting in the front room. They had the lights out so as not to attract outside attention, although it was getting close to when the city would start to stir.

The PDF cars were still outside Lasher's house, their lights still turning, red-yellow, red-yellow. It was hypnotic. One of the car's lights was starting to dim, spinning a little slower, the car battery draining. They had been there now for a long time.

The big men in the room were enforcers. Two sat near the front door and one near the opening to the back room and back door. They didn't participate in the conversation, and they each kept their eyes on the doors and windows.

Thomasito was talking in English. "They showed up right after you left. Our two worlds are colliding." He was explaining about the Columbians. "Sure enough, right after we talked about it, these *pendejos*—sorry, *el stupidos*—showed up. I didn't think much of it. We deal with them from time to time."

He looked down at his hands, holding them open and turning them over. "I was the *el stupido*. I brought them into the house but didn't go get my boys. They said they wanted to talk about business. I wanted to be a *gran hombre*, a big man. We started talking. Maria brought us some drinks. My daughter was playing with blocks. *Right here*."

Lasher just waited; he pretty much knew what the story was going to be but letting Thomasito tell it. Working through the anger would help what had to happen next.

Thomasito got up, then sat back down. It was the first time Lasher noticed that he wasn't moving right, so he asked, "Are you okay? You're moving slow."

Looking at Lasher directly, Thomasito replied, "They put me in a chokehold. I passed out. Made me feel weak." He regrouped his thoughts, looking at his hands again, now in fists. "Just like we talked about, they wanted to know why we weren't pushing Panama Red. Said it was business, and we had to earn."

He stood up again, agitated.

"Who do these asshats think they are? We don't earn for them. Damn Columbians, they think they own Panama now. Noriega is supposed to be strong, but he's looking down, not up. He is a big man with us Panamanians who can't fight back, but he is a mouse to Pablo's lion."

Pablo Escobar. The charismatic leader of the Columbian Medellín Cartel. He supplied cocaine to the world, bringing in over twenty-five million dollars a day through his global distribution. His cartel was in almost every country in South America and working their way north.

"I told them pretty much that, and the mood turned. We started to argue, threatening to move in here to the neighborhood." Thomasito looked at Alvarez, both men puffing their chests out, showing they were tough and would stand up to any intruder in their territory.

Thomasito said to Lasher, "They said I could choose between my family or theirs. One dude got behind me before I realized what was happening. Then I woke up, and everyone was gone, Maria and Sofia." He held back tears, too tough to let them show, but deeply distressed, putting his arm across his mouth.

Lasher looked at Cruz, then back to unconscious Williams. "Do you know where they took them?"

Thomasito flashed anger. "If I knew where they were, I would be there now, *man,* ripping apart the Columbian *naco* that took them and bringing my family home."

Lasher said in an understanding voice, "I know, Tomas. We'll get them back. Those DEA agents we dealt with yesterday will know where the Columbians are. I'm scheduled to meet with Walker at the hospital this morning."

They all sat in silence for a while, Thomasito getting up to walk around, then sitting back down a couple times.

After about twenty minutes, the lights stopped flashing outside, the PDF driving away.

Cruz got up to look out the window, watched them leave, then turned and said back to the room, looking at Lasher but talking to Thomasito and Alvarez also, "There are such things as coincidences"—he was leading up to something—"but this ain't that."

He walked back over to the chair he had been sitting in.

"Look. I'm on the outside, right? I can see everything with fresh eyes."

Both Lasher and Thomasito looked at him, interested.

"There is some kind of significant power move being made here. There is no way that Noriega had the PDF start eliminating American agents, across projects, at the exact same time that the Columbians began applying pressure to expand their in-country narcotics distribution of the most addictive drug combination in history. Both randomly happening at the same time on the first day of the new year.

"A friendly Panama could triple Pablo's already substantial distribution. Right now, it's almost all moved out of the country by plane. Panama, with the canal, could deliver a maritime distribution system. A hundred or more ships a day, coming and going. Unlike the planes we can track with radar, the ships will be invisible in plain sight."

Thomasito nodded. It made sense.

Lasher nodded and thought. "Wait," he said, still trying to piece everything together. "At twenty-five million dollars a day, what's got to be the biggest logistic? It's not moving the product. It's laundering the frigging money.

"You can move products in secret. You can't spend that kind of money in secret."

Cruz quickly responded, "If they are going to triple distribution, that's not just product. They will triple their income or more. Good Lord, that's going to be seventy-five to a hundred million dollars a day. Is there that much money in the world?"

Lasher kept thinking. Thomasito and Alvarez watched, interested.

This was big-time stuff. No wonder the DEA was in the country.

No wonder they were collecting this information for the US.

Before Lasher could finish his thoughts, Thomasito interjected, "I don't like it."

Cruz was in the moment. "None of us like it."

"No, *friend*." Thomasito got a profoundly serious look on his face. "If it is all this big, me and my family are small potatoes. We're not going to be that important to them. They will just move in here; they don't need us. I will never see Emily or Sophia again."

Cruz got a weird look on his face. "I'm…" He was struggling with something, a realization of what Thomasito said.

Lasher responded, not understanding Cruz's pause, "No one's family is small potatoes," using the same term, "everything comes down to family."

Lasher was angry at a level he had not been for some time. Maybe since his mom's death when he was little. Maybe never this angry; he knew how things worked now. He didn't when he was a kid.

Panama Red was evil, sure, but the people around it were worse. They used people up, spent life like spare change.

Lasher looked back at the two girls sitting with Williams. They were not going to lose a niece.

He looked at Thomasito, a big tough guy holding back tears behind red bloodshot eyes. He would not lose a wife and daughter.

The spark was at the forefront, Lasher's eyes so bright that Thomasito had difficulty holding his gaze. "I get it, Tomas. Principles and honor don't feed your kids, but you bank it anyway.

"It's your personal currency.

"We're going to get your family back.

"Today. We're going to send a message that the kangaroo is off-limits.

"Too expensive.

"They whisper with their words; we are going to shout loudly with our actions."

He thought about Grandpa Lasher. Having lost a daughter nearly broke him. Maybe it did. He thought about what it felt like when he lost his mom, eyes bright and full of anger.

"We're going to go get all of our families back from them and make them pay for their arrogance."

BREAKFAST

"Diederik!" Grandpa Lasher was calling for him.

Little Dirk looked up from his work. He was digging the Panama Canal and was at a precarious point. The central water reserve he had built (a hole he dug in the backyard and was filling with water from a hose) was near the breach.

The canal had been installed around a local village, a dangerous design that Dirk had warned the engineers about. They were going to have a meeting to discuss, but as Grandpa always said, "You can talk your way into a mess, but rarely out."

There were real lives at stake! (There were no real lives at stake.)

If he didn't get the main water flow redirected before the reserve filled, the entire town would be wiped out! Dirk knew he had to act fast. He just wasn't sure what to do.

Suddenly the water stopped. The reserve slowly drained into the ground.

A miracle! The town was saved!

He was probably in trouble, though; you came when Grandpa called the first time.

So, saving the town meant getting into trouble. Got it.

Fritz was barking, which meant Grandpa was getting worked up. This Fritz was new. He didn't know all the tricks the other Fritz had learned. He barked at Grandpa a lot, which Dirk worried about but Grandpa seemed to think was funny.

Dirk got up and tried to wipe the mud off his clothes, but he was covered in it. His hands were covered in it, so the more he wanted to get it off, the more he just spread it around and worked it into his shirt. Weird.

Grandpa had turned the hose off and was standing on the back porch. Fritz was barking at someone else—a big man, like Grandpa, standing next to him.

Dirk started to walk back to the house. The other big man was actually Fritz. He wasn't barking; he was yelling in German.

When Dirk was close enough, Grandpa looked at him and said, "Diederik, I'm tired of listening. They scream lies in whispers."

Fritz started yelling louder, the German sounding

harsh and short.

Dirk didn't understand but kept walking forward even though he noticed he wasn't getting any closer.

"The more this guy talks," Grandpa said, looking right at him and pointing at Fritz, Dirk suddenly on the porch looking up at him, "the more I miss my dog."

Lasher's head bounced forward; he startled awake, having fallen asleep on Thomasito's couch. He felt fatigued.

The sun was rising. He looked at a wall clock. It was 7:00 a.m. He must have been asleep for a couple hours. He felt terrible. His forehead and cheek hurt on his left side, his left arm hurt in a couple places too. He lifted his right arm to his forehead and felt a bandage. Same with his cheek and with his left arm. His shirt was off; a light sheet was on him. The cat scratch itched.

Thomasito's three large friends were still in the room, in the exact same position as at 4:00 a.m., two by the front door and one by the back.

Lasher's shirt was next to him. It had been cut off, one side bloody and ripped. There were two T-shirts next to it, both extra-large. One was pink and said *Bun in the oven* in Spanish with an arrow pointing down. The other shirt was gray and said *I'm with stupid* in English, with an arrow pointing up.

It wasn't that Lasher was picky. The gray shirt would blend in better; it was an excellent tactical color. He reached over, feeling the tape and bandage on his arm pull with the stretch, grabbing the gray shirt and then pulling it over his head, standing as he did so.

The two big men in the front of the room watched him. After he finished pulling the shirt over his head, one of the men handed the other a five-dollar bill. Nothing else was said, and they stayed serious, back to watching the front of the house.

Lasher realized he was hungry and that something smelled good.

He walked to the back to find Thomasito and Cruz eating breakfast. Eggs and potatoes. Williams was still asleep on the couch in the back room. Lasher turned around and went back to get the pink shirt, grabbed it, tossed it on Williams's sleeping form, then sat down at the table.

From nowhere, one of Thomasito's sisters showed up, putting a coffee cup down on the table and a plate full of eggs and potatoes.

"*Thank you,*" Lasher said in Spanish. He said it to the girl, then repeated it to Thomasito.

Lasher knew the culture and knew that he was receiving Thomasito's generosity. It was offered as a sincere courtesy. The proper social response was to accept it and be profusely humble in thanking him, so he could wave it off and not accept the gratitude. This was Thomasito's chance to "be a big man," like he talked about before. He would be drawing great pride from having enough food to give to guests. It was a sign of status as much as anything else.

After thanking him, Lasher said, "Tomas, thank you also for letting me sleep a couple hours. I need to be at the hospital by midmorning. This was time well spent."

Thomasito nodded.

Lasher continued. "*I hate to intrude further, but we have important work to do today. Do you have a brush and rag that I can use to clean my sidearm? Also, do you have any 9-millimeter ammunition? I would like to do a tactical reload.*"

An emergency reload was when the weapon was empty, and you needed to completely refill it. A tactical reload was when some rounds had been fired, and you wanted to restore to the maximum the weapon would carry.

Thomasito made a motion; one of the sisters left the room, presumably to get the items Lasher had asked for.

While waiting, Cruz leaned forward. "Chief, I'm supposed to be at PT right now."

"You're welcome," Lasher said quickly between bites, not looking up.

Cruz leaned back and smiled. "Yes, thank you. But

I'm technically AWOL."

Right, Lasher thought. *Cruz had finished his field time and was back on regular duty.* He looked at Thomasito.

"I need to get back into my house to use the phone. I imagine the place is trashed. Has there been any sign of the PDF since they left?"

Thomasito shook his head no. "I had a couple guys go over. It's trashed, yes. They didn't find bait traps. I think they were here last night on a smash-and-grab for you. My guys did say all your stuff was gone. I didn't think to have them see if the phone still worked."

Lasher nodded, disappointed because that meant he would be stuck in this stupid shirt all day.

"The phone is special. It's a secure line. As long as the main phone is still over there, and they didn't pull it out of the wall and take it, I can hook it back up."

Cruz stood up slowly, stretching. "Chief, I can go check and rewire it for you to save you some time."

Lasher shook his head, then paused. "Okay, but take some of Tomas's guys with you." He looked at Thomasito, who nodded his approval.

After Cruz left, Lasher asked, "Thomasito"—using his real name—"have you gotten any sleep?"

Thomasito was profoundly serious, the situation weighing on him. "I don't need sleep."

Lasher finished the plate of food. Out of nowhere, one of the sisters was there to take the plate, refill the coffee, and she placed a rag, oil, brush, and two different boxes of 9MM ammo on the table in exchange for the empty plate.

"Brother, trust me, this is going to be a long day. But it will end well if..." A pause. "*If* you get just a little rest, so you are fresh when we do what we have to do," Lasher said.

Thomasito nodded but did not move.

"If you become a liability," Lasher said to him in a commanding voice, as if talking to one of his soldiers, "because you're too stupid to rest when you can, you're not going with me." Lasher made a face that conveyed he was serious as he started to focus on disassembling his handgun for cleaning.

A flash of indignation crossed Thomasito's face, quickly followed by resignation, knowing Lasher was right.

Without looking up, Lasher continued. "I'll head out to the hospital in about two hours. I should be back here sometime late afternoon. I'll have the location we need when I come back. I need you to have at least two hours of sleep. After that, collect all the weapons and ammunition you can get your hands on—anything. We'll take the best of it. Then pick your five best men and have them ready to go.

"Not your big friends there; they are strong but too big and too slow. We need jungle fighters.

Good with weapons and good close in. Fast. Mean. Stealthy."

Thomasito nodded, thinking, getting up to head to the couch.

"And smart," Lasher finished. "And able to follow my instructions without question. We're going to be doing soldier's work today, Thomasito," he said as he pulled the two bandages off of his face and cheek.

DEA

Walker was sitting up in a hospital bed with an IV running from a bag into his arm. He was reading a book and looked up when Lasher came in. Both of his eyes were black underneath. His nose was black and blue with some kind of splint on it. He had a bandage around his head.

"What do you need an IV for? Did you get dehydrated when you cried yourself to sleep last night?" Lasher said as he walked in.

As Walker turned his head, lifting his eyes up from the book, he almost smiled but winced instead when he saw Lasher's shirt. "I couldn't agree more with your shirt. Does the Army require warning labels on their officers now?"

"Neck still hurts?" Lasher asked in a more serious and sympathetic tone this time. When Thomasito hit him yesterday in the back of the head to knock him out, Lasher could see it was a brutal strike.

Walker put the book down. "Yes, the neck is the worst part. Pain shoots through it like lightning if I move my little toe wrong. About two hours ago, I sneezed. Let me tell you..." He trailed off.

"How's Citlai?" Lasher asked about the other agent he had knocked out. "I didn't see him on the list down at the entry station," Lasher said.

Walker grimaced. "They got him awake a couple hours after we got here, moving him to the military hospital on Albrook, the Air Force base. He has some work to do to get right. It will be a while."

Lasher had a flash of guilt but pushed it away. *These clowns came in like tough guys, and Citlai tried to hit me in the face and was going to do it again.* As Grandpa Lasher would tell him repeatedly if he lost a fight: *It doesn't matter who threw the first punch or why; it only matters who threw the last.*

He nodded to Walker and sat in a chair by the bed.

The room had bright, big windows on the wall. It was clean, and the floor smelled medicinal and had clearly recently been waxed.

As Lasher sat down, Walker looked at him. "We've got a group staged. We are going to hit *Los Bravos* tomorrow. It's a distribution site. We know there is intel there to the location of their main facility in the South."

Lasher looked at him. He needed to find out where Thomasito's wife and daughter might have been taken, but without letting Walker know why. "I'm ready and can be your liaison."

Walker nodded. "Thanks. Sorry again for how things started. It was my fault." Walker was taking responsibility, which suggested to Lasher that he had good character.

"Is *Los Bravos* the main Columbian distribution site? Do they have any other significant locations in the city? Do they use *Los Bravos* for any other activity?" Lasher asked the last question enough on point with the others to be reasonable.

"Sure," Walker said, closing his eyes for a minute. "They have cells operating all over the city and in the countryside. But all Panama Red flows through *Los Bravos* to get in. It's their primary staging area."

Los Bravos was a range of foothills about twenty miles north and east of Panama City. It was the beginning of the deeper jungle in the hilly interior.

I need to confirm if that's the likely location of Thomasito's wife and kid. Walker seems like a straight shooter; I'm going to have to risk asking him point-blank.

"Walker, I have a matter I need to clean up before I head out with your team. One of my informants' wife and daughter were taken yesterday by Columbians pushing Panama Red. Threatening him to start distributing it, taking my CI's family as leverage. Do you think *Los Bravos* is where the family would end up?"

Lasher waited, uneasy to see if Walker would help.

Walker didn't miss a beat. "There is a sex trafficking business that runs through it, yes. There is an insatiable demand for young girls. Really young, sick stuff. If they took a young girl and decided not to use her themselves"—he paused again to show disgust—"then she would move through *Los Bravos.* I would bet ten to one if it really was Colombians pushing Red that they aren't going to give the family back. How old was the girl?"

Lasher realized he didn't know. Thomasito said she was playing with blocks. That sounded young, so he guessed, not knowing much about kids, "Five or six, I think."

Walker made a sour face, leaning toward Lasher a little, wincing with the move. "Yep," he said glumly, "she is gonna end up back in Columbia, then somewhere bad. They have islands I hear about where rich dudes fly in to have sex with kids about that age, and a little older, so she'll get the whole tenure. Pablo makes billions on his cocaine, but he has a meaningful side business in sex trafficking where he makes millions with a lot less effort."

Lasher grimaced also. He knew about stuff like this, could imagine it but had never had to deal with it in any aspect of his life, personal or professional.

"You'll get a chance to look around there tomorrow," Walker said, trying to sound comforting even though it rang hollow.

"What do we know about *Los Bravos*?" Lasher asked.

"It's run by a man named Alex Roman, one of the captains who reports through the inner circle to Pablo. The two have a long history. Roman is completely loyal to Escobar." Only two or three people dealt with Pablo Escobar directly. Working with the inner circle was the equivalent of being made in the Italian mob.

Walker continued. "Alex is older, in his fifties. He is actually an outstanding administrator, well organized. Goes without saying he is ruthless, but lots of people can be ruthless. He is organized enough for it to mean something."

"Can I get a briefing on the geography and aerial photos of the site? I know I am just a liaison, but I might want to bring an analyst with me, and I want to review the Army lists for targets of opportunity."

Walker nodded. "Do you know where the DEA offices are on Howard?"

Howard Air Force Base was the largest US military installation on the north side of the canal, over the Bridge of the Americas. The bridge was built in 1962 and was interesting because, technically, it was the only object outside of the canal locks that touched both sides of the American continent. It was the only way, other than water, to move between the two continents, central and south.

"I do not. But I know the base well," Lasher said.

"It's easy," Walker said happily. "After the gate, go straight. The PX will be on your right after about a quarter-mile. Take the road after it on the same side. When you hit the administrative buildings, it's the third one on the left. There is no sign. Tell them Walker six-six-seven-seven sent you to talk to Jefferson on floor three. I'll call ahead, so they know you are coming."

Lasher nodded and stood up.

Before he could say anything, Walker smiled and said, "And please don't change your shirt before you get there."

Lasher smiled and left, feeling that he and Walker were on good terms. He stopped near the nurse's station, showed his badge, and used the desk phone there. He dialed the number for the general's driver.

A desk MP answered. Lasher identified himself and gave the pass code *SPC Mariana* the intelligence analyst currently pulling the duty he had talked to last night had given him. After a few moments, she came on the line.

"Specialist Mariana, how may I help you, sir or ma'am?" The standard enlisted duty phone greeting.

Lasher got right to it. "This is Chief Lasher. I have a field opportunity if you want it. Won't be through channels. You have three days off coming up, correct?" he asked.

"Yes, sir!" Mariana sounded thrilled.

"Specialist, what was your last PT rating?" Lasher needed to know she would be able to handle herself physically. She might be excited now at the chance for adventure, but the realities of fieldwork were much different than the analysts thought.

She didn't miss a beat in answering, "Two-forty-five."

That was a good score. Three hundred was the most you could score. A soldier needed one hundred eighty to pass. Two-forty-five was good but not great. Not for fieldwork.

"What was your two-mile?" he asked her.

"Eighteen-o-five, sir." Her voice had lost some of the confidence and excitement.

Eighteen minutes to run two miles would have failed a male soldier, but it was good on the female chart. The Army PT test consisted of three activities: pushups, sit-ups, and a two-mile run. The pushups measured upper body strength, the sit-ups' core body strength, and the run overall fitness. A two-forty or so score meant she had scored about eighty in each category out of a hundred.

In the field, though, there were no charts. Time

was time. Strength was strength. Still, two nine-minute miles, good upper body, reasonable core. It would work.

"Okay, that's a pass." He could sense the relief on the other end. "Specialist, once in the field, you may not get the chance to sleep for a while. Sleep now as much as you can. Force it if you must.

"Meet me tomorrow at 4:00 a.m. at the Albrook terminal by the runway, having had breakfast, taking care of your morning constitutional, being caffeinated if that is your thing, leaving nothing between you and a productive day."

"Yes, sir."

Lasher paused. "Wear civilian clothes, something that you can take to the jungle if we need to. Do you have a personal sidearm?"

A longer pause on the other end. "No, sir." Mariana's voice was now very serious, realizing, maybe for the first time, that fieldwork might not be the fantasy that the analysts sat around thinking it was.

"Okay, I'll find you something." Lasher hung up.

He wanted one of his own running ops for him during the DEA raid. Ops was a sophisticated military term meaning operations, but it really just meant that Mariana would be on the radio from a command station (probably the car they took to the area) along with the DEA agent's controllers.

This way, he stood a better chance of getting the data he needed and unscrewing things if it turned into a DEA operational cluster.

He made a mental note to get her a handgun from somewhere, but the rest of it would be for tomorrow. There was still a lot of work to do today.

As Lasher pulled out of the hospital, he got on *Balboa Avenue,* which would take him to the *Pan-American Highway* where he could head northwest and go over the Bridge of the Americas. As he drove, he allowed his frustration with Cruz to take the forefront of his thoughts.

Instead of fixing the phone in Lasher's house and leaving it at that, Cruz had claimed that as soon as he got it reconnected, it rang, so he answered it. He told Lasher it was Captain Crostino who ordered Cruz back to base. Cruz swore he wouldn't talk about what had gone on last night since Williams was safe.

While Cruz reported to Lasher in the company hierarchy, that relationship was suspended when Lasher was in the field. Technically, however, it was still bad form to go around your direct supervisor. This was Cruz's second full in-country tour. He might be getting more comfortable here than he should. The Army moved soldiers around so much to keep their core frame of reference the military hierarchy proper, not a local mindset. They wanted a soldier to always identify as a service member assigned somewhere, not someone who lived at a location and happened to have a job in the military.

A slight difference with a substantial psychological distinction.

Lasher didn't like the move in general, but it also sent up warnings on the edges. Not entirely sure what or why, other than it seemed there was a mole somewhere in the military chain given the housing situation, the repetitive usage of the same locations, and apparent PDF knowledge of the locations.

Lasher couldn't draw a straight line between that and Cruz, but an agent lived for opportunities like now to work a big case in the field. Even the analysts wanted in on it like Mariana. Either Cruz was stupid and really answered the phone, its own problem, or something else. It could be just cowardice, but Lasher had seen Cruz in action.

He mentally filed this away, too, focusing on the tasks at hand. The large bridge came into view. It had been modern in 1962 when it was built; now it looked old and industrial. Traffic moved at a good clip this time of day, heading over it in two lanes going in both directions.

The sun was out. Panama looked like a painting. As it was the end of the rainy season, everything was bright, healthy, and green. Many of the buildings were yellow with red clay tiles. The University of

Panama was on the right-hand side of the bridge on a small peninsula of land, its facilities organized and grand-looking.

As Lasher drove onto the bridge, he could see out to his left into the bay. Bright blue water with hundreds of ships spotted the bay and, farther out, awaited their turn to traverse the canal through the locks. To his right, he could see down the canal, the waterway forming a V as it transitioned from bay to canal—the first colossal set of locks, concrete structures painted white, raising and lowering ships.

The middle of the bridge went over the central channel, a deep trench dug leading from the bay to the locks. The water changed from blue to black over it, clearly visible from this height. Without the deep channel, the canal would be useless for anything other than the most modest seagoing vessels.

A common misunderstanding about the canal was that most people thought it was a single north/south structure built to span between the Caribbean Sea and the Bay of Panama. The canal actually ran northwest to southeast on an obtuse angle. While a good amount of the canal was dug out on the southern Panama City side, roughly half of the waterway was the man-made Gatun Lake. The canal exited on the northwest side at Colon, a much smaller city than Panama City.

As Lasher rounded the rise of the bridge, he could see the western areas sprawling before him, the bright blue sky contrasting the vivid greens and yellows of the natural surroundings. Panama was tropical, but its dominant vegetation looked more rainforest than the inland areas of southern Florida where Lasher grew up. More leafy trees than palm trees. Much hillier and lusher.

Panama City ended at the bridge; the western side was the complete opposite. There were no large urban sprawls, just jungle and much more modest construction. The Air Force base turn was a few minutes over the bridge, a left, and a small wind up to the guard station. The Air Force called their police security police (SP) compared to the Army's military police. The SPs and MPs fulfilled the same role across services.

Lasher was waved through and followed Walker's directions to the DEA administrative building.

Everything on all of the American bases looked the same, be it an Army post or airbase. The buildings all looked old. They were a cream color with red clay shingles on the roofs, built from cinder blocks.

It was an effective if boring, two-tone presentation.

Lasher parked his car outside the admin building and went inside.

The building looked just like all the others on the outside. If he had walked into this building not knowing its occupants, he might have assumed the building was not in usage. There was a completely empty wide and short entry area with a single door on the opposite wall from where he came in. He walked across the open space and pulled on the second door; it was locked.

He looked around and didn't see any other option, so he pulled on the door again. This time it opened with a buzzing sound.

They must have a monitored video surveillance system, Lasher thought to himself. It wasn't how the Army did things; the DEA was flush with budget money, which allowed them to make things much more complicated than they needed to be. If this were an Army building, there would be several MPs; they would challenge an unauthorized visitor.

Here it felt like the DEA would just hide from them behind their big, secured door. If there were a real problem, the agents inside would have to counter the threat emerging from a single point. Immediately entering the situation from a tactical disadvantage.

Lasher smirked at the thought that DEA agents were paid on average about four pay grades higher than military personnel. Higher pay for much less expertise.

The inside of the inner area on the other side of the door was a whole different world. There were cubicles and offices on the edges of the large room. A lot had gone into building this space out. Everyone had a computer workstation; there were several large meeting rooms with glass walls so you could see in and out. The rooms had large screens on a wall with a back-projected slide machine.

There was an overly attractive American woman at the reception desk. "Are you Chief Lasher?" She asked as Lasher entered and the security door closed behind him.

Classic feds, Lasher thought. *All this security and I get buzzed in before they know who I am or if I am allowed to even be in here.*

Instead of worrying about their problems, Lasher produced his badge. "Yes, ma'am. I am here to see —"

She cut him off with a smile, taking the badge and making notes in a log. "Yes, Agent Walker called and let us know you were on your way." She had a small thrill or something going on, her attractive face a slight flush.

She leaned forward, drawing Lasher in, then in a softer voice said, "Is it true you knocked out both Walker and Citlai by yourself? With just one move?"

Lasher smiled a thin smile, not revealing anything; the woman was flirting with him to get information. He didn't answer the question, so there was a moment of awkward silence. The woman was not used to applying her wares with no effect.

Finally, she leaned back, the artificial moment over, her tone changing to more businesslike. "The stairs are over there to your right. Jefferson is on the third floor in the first conference room on your left."

Lasher nodded a thank you and put his badge portfolio back in his rear pocket. Once the badge was in, he let his hand tap his Springfield sidearm, holstered right above his back pocket, a little surprised the DEA let him in with it.

The conference room was where she said it would be. There were two men in the room. One was clearly an analyst; the other was harder to guess, an athletic fit-looking man maybe in his late thirties. Lasher opened the glass door and entered the room, extending his hand to the closest person, presumably Jefferson, the analyst.

Both men stood up, and they all shook hands, the second man introducing himself as SAC Powers. He was the special agent in charge of the *Los Bravos* mission.

Powers indicated a seat to Lasher on the other side of the large table where they could see each other and where Lasher would have a good view of the presentation screen.

"Nice shirt. Would you like something to drink?" Powers asked Lasher, taking a sip from a coffee cup in front of him and pointing to a coffee station near the back of the room.

The DEA has it nice, Lasher thought as he nodded, got up, and made himself a cup of coffee. He wanted caffeine. It was good coffee; Lasher made an approving face when he took his first sip and sat back down.

Powers spoke up, clearly in the lead. Jefferson had yet to say anything other than his initial greeting.

"We've got our briefing loaded up on the projector," Powers said. "Is there anything specific you want us to touch on, or do you just want a general overview of the mission?"

"I know I'm in a back-seat role here, but I would like a detailed overview of the layout and any known high-value targets that will be on-site. I want to run through the Army targets-of-opportunity list, both black and gray, just in case."

Lasher was not going to be able to run the list through normal channels. He would have to get SPC Mariana to run it before she lost access to the computer system when her shift as the general's driver ended in a few hours. Additionally, he needed an excuse to get as much information as possible to the layout to try and identify where Thomasito's family might be held. He wasn't single-minded, though. He wanted to take down the facility, arrest Alex Roman, and get the location of the production facility so they could take it out.

He suspected that the DEA already knew where the

production facility was. They would have satellites easily capable of locating it. The raid tomorrow on *Los Bravos* was either a confirmation or something else.

We're both going to be working our own angles tomorrow, he thought about Powers. *But we have the same endgame in mind. I need to figure out if Powers is capable before I leave here.*

Jefferson dimmed the room lights with a knob on the table, so the rear-projection screen was easier to see. He had a clicker in his hand that seemed to control the rear slide machine located behind the wall without a wire.

The first slide up was a photo of Alex Roman. Roman was a good-looking, tall westerner. Lasher had expected a Columbian.

Jefferson began speaking while flipping through several photos of Roman in different settings.

"Alex Roman was born in 1948 in Georgia. He grew up in an orphanage at Our Sainted Mother outside of Columbus near the Alabama-Georgia state line."

Click, Roman in jungle gear executing what looked like a fellow contra.

Click, Roman drinking wine at an upscale-looking villa.

"By the age of seventeen, he was running three different low-level enterprises. Taking protection money from the farmers to make sure their crops got to market, an underground gambling ring in Columbus proper, and he was a pimp for at least twenty of the girls from the orphanage."

Click. Another slide. Roman was on a podium speaking to what looked like about a thousand jungle fighters.

"By twenty-one, he had been to the Macon County lockup twice. Convicted of a double homicide when he was twenty-four, he escaped when the transporting vehicle moving him from the courthouse to the prison was ambushed."

Click. Newspaper headlines about the attack.

"In 1976, he showed up in Columbia, helping Escobar found the Medellín Cartel. Since Roman looked American, he initiated several of the smuggling routes into the US. He ran, from what we know, powder into Texas for three years in the seventies."

Click. Roman and Escobar are at a pool somewhere drinking ridiculous tropical drinks surrounded by women in different states of clothing.

Click. About fifteen soldiers stripped and hung upside down from trees in the jungle, Roman yelling something at more live captives on the ground.

Click. The same scene later, with all of the captive soldiers dead, many butchered with missing limbs.

A horror show.

"As a reward for time well served, Escobar put him

in charge of *Los Bravos*. It's a semi-retirement. He has been in-country for the past three years. The facility is only just now growing in importance again as the Medellín Cartel formed an agreement with Noriega to come in under his protection."

Click. A satellite image of *Los Bravos.*

The compound was about what Lasher expected. It was not as large a facility as it was an important one, which was lucky.

Jefferson produced a laser pointer from somewhere. The image on the slide showed a roughly half-circular military-style layout. There were nine structures with well-used paths between the buildings. The facility backed up to a hill with a high rough wall. Good strategic thinking for defense, only having to defend from anyone approaching from one-hundred-eighty degrees, not three-sixty.

Everything is a trade-off, though. That's an excellent defensive position, but there is no escape route for retreating, Lasher thought to himself. *Of course, the culture of the cartels and Narcotraficante, in general, would not see this as a downside. Instead, probably as an upside. Built-in motivation.*

There were guard positions at four places around the half-circle curve extending out from the hill wall. The areas approaching the facility were from a slightly lower elevation and had been cleared of vegetation for roughly fifty yards out in all directions.

"Roman is at the facility at *Los Bravos* almost one hundred percent of the time. He drives south along the American Intercontinental Highway about once a week to Yaviza, where we lose him for about five hours. Yaviza has a population of nearly five thousand people.

"We take his disappearance to mean that about two hours further east into the start of the Darien Gap is where the main grow location is. He spends about an hour there making sure everything is running as planned, then returns."

The Darien Gap marked the continental divide between Central America and South America. The center of it was the border between Colombia and Panama. It was largely unpassable, a combination of a dense rain forest, high mountain peaks, and a large water divide.

The geography made it "possible" to cross from Columbia into Panama with a lot of work. It was near impossible to return that way. This was another reason the Darien Gap would be a strategic location for Escobar; it was outside the Colombian government's reach. He could send people there from Columbia. If he could secure transport through the Panama Canal, he would have massively improved distribution.

Escobar made his money selling powdered cocaine. Crack was made by cooking the powder with baking soda. Lacing it into marijuana was a brilliant business move, if an abhorrent moral one. Panama Red was the result. Almost immediately addictive, used by casual and serious users alike. It could be a game-changer to an already powerful position.

"The Darien Gap?" Lasher asked. "I thought that it was mostly an impassable dense jungle."

Powers smirked. "That's exactly what it is. There are still native tribes living there like it was a thousand years ago. It's some of the most unforgiving jungle on the entire planet."

Click. The same overhead photo of the compound but zoomed in to bring the center into clarity.

"We know these two buildings are small barracks." The laser pointer identified two buildings near the back. "This is where Roman lives and works." A square building near the middle; it had a pool but did not look like a house. "These are warehouses and storage." All but one building had been identified.

"What is the building up there in the corner?" Lasher asked. *That has got to be where they keep the women.*

Jefferson looked to Powers. Powers nodded to go ahead.

"They always have five or six women available to the soldiers. That is where they keep them," Jefferson said.

Lasher repositioned in his chair. "That's a pretty big building for five or six prostitutes," he said.

Powers made a motion with his hand to Jefferson, suggesting he get on with it and stop wasting time.

"I didn't mention…" Jefferson looked uncomfortable. "When Roman goes to Yaviza each week, it is usually in a caravan with several other vehicles. Behind them almost always is an old, converted school bus. Looks just like a normal *red devil*."

The Red Devils were the nickname used to describe the thousands of converted school busses into quasi-public transportation systems. Painted as flamboyantly as possible, these buses were the primary method for the local people to move around the city and the country.

Jefferson continued, "We figure he moves about eight to fifteen girls a week."

"What about a woman they captured in her twenties? What would happen to her?" Lasher asked.

Jefferson didn't miss a beat, now back to his full analyst role with Powers having given him permission to disclose all of the necessary intel. "If they could dope her up and she didn't fight too much, she would live here"—he indicated the ninth building structure—"for a while as a prostitute. Maybe three or four months between surviving the amount of dope they would keep in her system and the soldiers getting bored with her and wanting to make room for a newer..." He struggled for a word. "Newer...acquaintance."

Clumsy language, but it got the point across.

Lasher turned to Powers. "Is tomorrow a smash-and-grab for intel, a target and destroy, psychological?"

A military raid could have one of about seven primary missions. Everything from demoralizing an enemy, destroying/killing assets, freeing captives, capturing high-value targets, or collecting information. Or any combination of those basic objectives.

"It's a smash-and-grab," Powers answered. "We really don't know where the grow facility is, but we believe that there are maps in Roman's villa. The paperwork he would give to a new driver, nothing that they would see as high value. That's priority one. A secondary objective is to cause enough damage to slow operations down for at least a couple days.

"We're not worried about alerting them down in the Darien Gap. Once we have a solid fix on the position of the grow fields, we have 830th Air Division lined up with ten refitted UH-60s. Once we know where it is, we're simply going to destroy it and the surrounding area from the air."

The UH-60 was a four-blade, twin-engine, medium-lift helicopter commonly referred to as a

"Black Hawk." A refitted UH-60 doubled its missile profile. Ten UH-60s would undoubtedly be enough to devastate several square miles of rainforest.

"So, tomorrow's intel raid is the entire mission outline," Lasher stated, and Powers nodded. He tried to keep it as a casual follow-on. "And a couple days after, you will hit the fields on the Darien Gap. Once their location can be confirmed by satellite." Also stated as a fact.

Powers nodded. "Yep, another win for the good guys." The tension of the briefing had passed, but he continued, wrapping up. "We're going in tomorrow at noon, in broad daylight. Sending a message. We're taking three Little Birds. It's a ten-man team, eleven counting you."

The Little Bird was a small six-person helicopter gunship: two crew and four passengers, usually a Boeing MH-6 model. However, the Air Force had several modified AH-6s they could use for the same mission. The AH-6 was modified and more attack-oriented.

"You leave from Albrook, pre-flight and briefing is 7:00 a.m.

"We're expecting around twenty soldiers and a few civilians. You'll get the tactical brief tomorrow morning from SA Hutch. He is leading the assault," Powers finished.

"You're not leading it?" Lasher asked, caught off guard.

Powers smiled. "My field days are behind me."

Lasher found that hard to believe. Powers was not that old, and he looked to be in almost as good a condition as Lasher was.

"Will you be running OPS?" Lasher asked.

"Yes." Powers smiled again. "Do you want to see our mission management center?"

Lasher also smiled, both men getting up from the table. "Of course I would." He was genuinely interested in seeing how the DEA operations worked.

I also need to understand how much insight they will have to the side operation I need to run, Lasher thought. *If Powers turns out straight, I'm tempted to tell him I need to include the equivalent of a hostage rescue.*

The problem is if I ask him and he says no, then Thomasito is out of luck.

He didn't have anyone he could consult with, and letting Powers know about Thomasito's family could go in any direction. The worst was that Powers waited a day or two and found another Army liaison.

All three exited the conference room; Powers led them down a long hallway. At the end was a door to a closed-off room, not the clear open office Lasher had observed downstairs and up here on the third floor.

Powers punched in a code on the door and pulled it

open. When the door opened, the lights turned on by themselves. There was no one in the large room. There were three rows of tables with computers at them. Each station had a headset sitting on the keyboard and a phone.

The front of the room had four giant screens. Lasher looked up and could see a projector on the back wall, one for each screen.

Powers looked up with him. "We have access to several NSA and CIA databases in real time for research and can project satellite feeds here and here." He pointed to the two middle projection screens.

"We'll have live comms tomorrow, and two satellites will be over, so we'll be able to observe from here in near real time," Power finished proudly.

Lasher was genuinely impressed. "All this to catch pot dealers?"

"And people who take the tags off their beds, yes," Powers responded good-naturedly.

They will be able to see anything I have Thomasito do with this setup. I'm going to have to risk it. If he says no, I'll figure something out.

"Powers, can I talk to you for a moment?" Lasher asked as nicely as he could but kept his tone sounding professional.

Powers nodded, then when Lasher didn't do anything, he nodded again. "Jefferson, can you give us a minute?"

Jefferson nodded and left the room. He looked relieved to be able to get back to how he usually spent his time.

When he was gone, Lasher leaned against one of the tables, relaxing, which suggested to Powers that he was being more casual. "I have a hypothetical for you."

Powers sat in one of the desk chairs. It was on wheels and swiveled easily. It looked comfortable. He nodded his head, indicating that Lasher could continue.

"I have a CI that had his wife and daughter grabbed late last night. I have every reason to believe they will be moved through the *Los Bravos* compound. I believe they will be there tomorrow when your operation starts."

He looked at Powers, who was listening intently but not giving anything away.

That's enough for now; let's see what he says.

Powers waited a bit longer, then realized Lasher was waiting for a comment. "We've been planning this for a while. With just ten operatives, securing the villa and Roman are about as far stretched as I am comfortable with. It is already two-to-one."

He's open. I just need to make it so it's not his problem.

"I've got one of my teams ready," Lasher said confidently. Of course, he didn't. He was operating on the edge of his authority having only Thomasito and however many Panamanian street thugs Thomasito could round up that passed Lasher's scrutiny.

Powers made a face of impressed surprise. "Is this sanctioned?"

Lasher nodded that it was. It wasn't, but the bluff passed.

"Then what do you need from me?"

Lasher leaned forward. *I need to tell him the truth, or at least enough of it to convince him. I'm going to have to embellish a little here.*

"I need two things. If you hadn't shown up when you did, I planned on taking my team in by jeep tomorrow. That can't work now with your schedule. I don't want to go back later after your operations. If I can't get there before, it would be a mess. Our two targets and timings line up.

"So, what I need is for you to add another Little Bird for my team."

Powers waited again. "That's one thing. What's the other?"

Lasher smiled, realizing Powers was not going to say no. "I guess that's it, just one thing." He stood up, and the two men shook hands.

"Can I use a secure phone line?" Lasher asked, wanting to call Mariana so she could run the target lists.

Powers smiled. "Sure, you can use a phone in here. I guess it was two things after all."

PX

L asher drove the short distance from the DEA building to the Air Force base PX.

I just told Powers that I have a team ready to go. I'm going to have to make Thomasito and his guys look the part.

He flashed his military ID to the greeter at the door. The PX was large and had aggressive air conditioning. The temperature inside was seventy-two degrees, almost thirty degrees cooler than the outside. He felt the wall of cold hit him. Somehow it made the cat scratch itch even more.

When he walked in, there was a little room off to his right that sold computers. He walked past it knowing exactly where he wanted to go. He grabbed a shopping cart and headed straight to the surplus section of the store in the back right corner. They sold everything from weapons and ammunition to fatigues, boots, survival equipment, and field rations.

He bought himself a new shirt, this one a thin long-sleeved T-shirt that was light and dark gray. Not exactly camo, but a good color to blend into almost any environment. He grabbed three of the same shirts in each of its different sizes, having no idea who Thomasito would find to help from his side and wanting to be covered. He grabbed some kids' clothes, just random stuff, but it might come in handy.

He also put jungle boots for himself in the cart and grabbed a boxed P226 for Mariana along with ten boxes of ammunition. He found several jungle hats, two large hunting knives, a box of field rations, a radio kit with two hand units and four field-quality headsets, canteens, hair clippers, a handful of iodine tablets, and finally, he got a rugged backpack.

We're going to need to look like a unit. He thought about it and went back and grabbed four more of the boxed P226s and more 9MM ammunition.

As he was wheeling his cart to checkout, he got a few snickering looks. Lasher just smiled back at them; their assumption that he was a PX warrior was pretty far off. He grabbed a few food items on the way out, throwing them almost randomly into the basket. As he was waiting in line, Lasher ran down his checklist.

I have a lot to do to pull this off, he thought to himself. *The hardest part is going to be keeping Thomasito calm and focused. He will not be happy when he first sees his wife. She is being passed around even now. And the child? My god, if they are doing what I think they are doing to her, it will be hard to keep Thomasito under control.*

The cashier rang everything up. It came to over a thousand dollars; he used his personal credit card. Lasher didn't spend any of his own money very often, instead having ninety percent of his twice-monthly pay deposited into a savings account. Since he enlisted, he had been doing this and had substantial savings already—ten years of military pay primarily untouched.

He told the checkout lady that he didn't need any bags and wheeled the cart out to his car near the back of the parking lot. When he got to it, he changed shirts. He put everything else in his trunk, taking it out of the shopping cart and stuffing everything into two military duffle bags.

The drive back took about an hour. It was getting on to 3 p.m. The day was clear; the sky was blue. Panama was still hot. Well into the nineties, the humidity had broken, which made it feel significantly cooler compared to just yesterday, even though the temperatures were about the same.

He pulled into the alley behind Thomasito's house an hour later.

Now he had to deal with Williams.

CHOICES

Cruz was gone. Williams was awake; he and Lasher talked for a bit. Williams ran through everything he could remember, confirmation of what Lasher already thought had happened. Confirming he had gone to drop off his stuff at the condo where they grabbed him. He had a car he thought should still be at the building in the above-ground parking structure.

Williams was beaten badly. It looked like the PDF had used a combination of physical discomfort and some mild truth-like-serum drug. Williams had nothing to tell them of any real importance, so Lasher wasn't worried.

"I'm good, Dirk," Williams said, his dark skin hiding more bruises than he was admitting to.

"I'm going to need you tomorrow, Jack. Do you feel up to it? I want to use you as ops. We're going to hit a big target attached to a DEA operation; we'll need our own CIC, even if it's just you on the radio in a car parked close by." CIC stood for Combat Information Center.

Lasher ran down a summary of the DEA operation and the information they had given him.

Once Lasher had finished, Williams was still skeptical. "How big are the operations at *Los Bravos?*" he asked.

Lasher thought, then, "From what I could gather, it's the most important Panama Red distribution location this side of the canal." His face got serious. "But they run stuff both ways. Panama Red in, females out, to be sold off as, well, sex slaves."

They were quiet for a few moments; this was a heavy subject. Tough to get your head around in today's modern age.

Finally, Williams spoke. "How are you and a handful of Tomas's guys gonna arrest fifty Columbian *Narcotraficante* and sex traffickers?"

He doesn't understand what I am going to do. He is still thinking like an enlisted soldier, not a field agent.

Lasher dropped his shield and talked to Williams man to man. "Jack, they took this man's family, his wife, his daughter. They told him he would get them back only if he brought their poison into his neighborhood and sold it to children.

"But instead, the people they took are going to be sold and used up. A good mother and a little kid.

"On top of that, these Columbian *Narcotraficante* are working with Noriega, with the PDF. They tried to capture me and did capture you. If they got their way, everyone in this house would be dead, enslaved, or imprisoned.

"Including you.

"Crostino isn't going to do anything about it. She's bucking for major. The way to get promoted is to not have any problems. This sure as heck is a big set of problems."

Williams made a face of recognition, so he kept going.

"You and I never talked much. That's okay. I don't know why you joined. I joined up because it was the best way I could think to make a difference in people's lives. If this isn't that…" There was a short pause. "Well, this *is* that. This is our chance to make a real difference."

Williams sat up straight, engaging in the conversation. "So, what are you going to do?" He slowly understood the scope and magnitude of what Lasher had planned.

"I am going to get Tomas's family back." Lasher looked him square in the eye.

"You're going to have to kill several dozen people to do it," Williams said. It wasn't accusatory. He was resigning to it, doing his own internal processing. Lasher could tell Williams would not be making the same choices that Lasher was.

That's why we started off as peers, and now you have

to salute me, Lasher thought to himself.

It wasn't a put-down of Williams or pride about his position. Instead, resolute introspection at how a person's worldview could affect their decision-making. It was essential to know yourself and have meaningful goals.

"It's gonna be a bloody mess." Williams was still processing the conversation.

A small wave of either anger or frustration rose in Lasher. He snapped back, "It's already a bloody mess."

"This isn't really our charter, Dirk." Williams was now trying to be reasonable, to negotiate his way out by appealing to a higher authority. "We're low-level collectors, observe and report. We collect pieces of a puzzle, but we don't even know what kind of puzzle it is, much less what the picture is. We should just do our job and let the higher-ups figure all this out."

"They made me the DEA liaison for their in-country operations."

"Liaisons don't necessarily lead alternate raids."

"What do you want to do, not save the kids?"

Williams looked sincere, almost pleading. "Save them by collecting their whereabouts and reporting them!"

"To who? The PDF is in bed with the Columbians; the DEA doesn't care it isn't their mission; the

Army brass doesn't care; it has nothing to do with them."

"It had nothing to do with the Army because Panamanian hostages held by Columbians are not a part of protecting U.S. interests."

Lasher paused; Williams was wrong. "Jack, protecting the innocent and vulnerable from the corrupt and powerful—that *is* our interest. If we can't do that, then what is the point of any of it? For me, the United States means doing what's right. Being united. I am an officer; these people are my interest." He shook his head, near giving up.

Lasher tried one more time even though he didn't think Williams was listening anymore. "Tomas is going in there if I go with him or not. Which do you think is better? Which way do you think that little girl stands a stronger chance of not spending the next three years of her life as a doped-up sex slave, then getting strangled in her sleep because she is no longer worth more than the cost of the food that keeps her alive?"

Thomasito was standing in the kitchen doorway. Lasher had not seen him there and was surprised, wishing he had not heard the last remark, frustrated with himself for caring if he convinced Williams or not.

"We're ready, *jefe*," was all Thomasito said as he returned to the living room.

VOLUNTEERS

There were eight men total in the room when Lasher and Williams walked in. Thomasito, the three big guys who had been guarding the place since yesterday, and four sturdy-looking men, presumably the one's Lasher had asked him to gather.

Thomasito was sitting on the edge of the couch, on the armrest. They had left the larger chair, the one Thomasito usually sat in, for Lasher. Between that and Thomasito calling Lasher *jefe,* meaning boss, it seemed that the Panamanians here in the room, probably under Thomasito's order, were going to allow him to lead them.

Lasher remained standing, looking over each man. There was an eclectic assortment of weapons on display, everything from machetes to two old MP5 submachine guns.

"*I have good news,*" he addressed the group. Each person in the room was watching him intently.

"*Four of us are going in by helicopter alongside a DEA task force.*

"*Tomas, it will be you, me, and you can pick your best two other men here. Let me give you the full briefing, then you can decide.*

Lasher went back to the kitchen, grabbed a handful of paper plates, and then returned, laying them out. "*We're taking gunships to their facility. It's in the foothills of Los Bravos, about thirty miles from here.*"

He started to lay out the paper plates on the floor based upon the satellite images he had seen, using the couch as the large hill the compound backed up to.

"*The couch here is a tall cliff face, the back of their compound. I think this building here*"—he indicated the back building where he had been told the females were kept—"*is where we will find both Emily and Sophia are being held. There will be others, from what I have been told, five or six other older women and as many as ten or fifteen children.*"

Lasher looked up from his impromptu map to make sure everyone was following, then he continued.

"*The DEA isn't going to care about these people. I am going to have Williams back here and another soldier bring a car big enough for everyone.*

"*There are defensive positions here, here, here, and here.*" He pointed to places on the perimeter. "*They have machine gun mounts. The gunships will try and take them out on our way in.*"

One of the faces Lasher didn't recognize, a younger teenager, stood up and said, "This is crazy, man. Thomasito, I want to show you nothing but respect, but I can't do this. I don't want to go to war with the Americans." The kid started to walk for the front door.

Lasher made a motion to one of the big guys, who saw it and blocked the door.

Turning to Thomasito, Lasher said, "*Tomas, I need everyone here to stay here until tomorrow afternoon unless they come with us. We can't risk word getting out and giving the enemy advanced warning.* Everyone stays here, and no one uses the phone." He said the last part in English.

Thomasito nodded, angry in general and staring down at the kid.

"Our gunship is going to land here." He indicated an open area by the back building he had identified. "The DEA team is going to land here, here, and here."

Before Lasher could continue, Thomasito asked, "*Jefe, why would the Americans and the DEA help me?*"

The question was reasonable, but Lasher was not ready for it. Thomasito looked terrible, a combination of angry and feeling helpless.

I didn't consider how this might look from his stand-point; I need to remember to better explain how I got all this set up. Especially when I let them know they will be pretending to be American soldiers. But we can get to that after everything else has been ironed out. This is a tightrope.

Lasher looked at him, a flash memory crossing his mind of driving home from the hospital the night his mother finally died, looking at Grandpa —a man he only vaguely knew—and being afraid. He had asked Grandpa Lasher the same question.

Grandpa, is being dead forever?

His grandfather had looked at him. *Yes, Dirk. I'm sorry; your mom is gone. She is not coming back.*

Ever? Little Dirk asked.

A pause. *No, I'm sorry. Not ever.*

Who is going to take care of me?

Grandpa's big, strong hand patted his head. *I am going to take care of you, Dirk.*

Why? A natural question from a child.

Because we are family. It's what family does.

But Thomasito and I are not family, Lasher thought in the here and now. *How do I explain I am doing this as much for myself as for them? I'll describe it to him as best I can.*

Lasher answered, "Thomasito, I lost my mom

when I was very young. I never knew my father. I know what an unexpected loss of family feels like. I vowed in my life to help keep anyone else from having to endure that feeling if there was anything I could do about it."

I might as well deal with this next part; they won't be more open to it than right now.

"There is more to this, though. It's not all good-will." Lasher walked over to the window, a habit he had when he was thinking deeply.

"As far as the DEA knows, you are my team of US Army commandos. They know the truth about what we need to do, but I was a little vague on some of the details."

"*Jefe, I appreciate the help*," Thomasito said earnestly, looking around the room, "*but hoss, we don't look anything like American soldiers*."

It was true they did not.

"I have a solution for that. First, Tomas, it's going to be you and me. We can only bring two other people. Who do you want it to be?"

Thomasito looked at his friends. Other than the kid, they all wanted to help. They obviously knew Maria and Sofia and wanted to assist in getting them back.

"Leo and Julian, you two are coming with us," Thomasito said. Both men looked relieved. "Diego"—the third man—"I need you to stay here and keep my house safe."

Smart, Lasher thought. *That's good leadership. Everyone gets something to do so they can feel like they are contributing.*

Lasher walked over to his two duffle bags and dumped them onto the floor, next to the make-shift map he had made. He tossed shirts like the one he was currently wearing to each of the men identified as going on the raid. He also gave the P226s to Thomasito, Leo, Julian, and Williams and two ammo boxes each. He kept the last P226 to the side. He would give that to Mariana tomorrow morning.

Everyone's eyes lit up. You would have thought it was Christmas morning, each person getting the gift they had been hoping for.

"Everyone gets a haircut, including me. We're going to look like a unit." Lasher unboxed the clippers he had bought and handed them to Williams. Most soldiers, by the time they re-upped their enlisted contract, had become proficient barbers with clippers. It was an easy way to save money on the constant need to keep your hair short and within regulation.

"Jack," Lasher said, looking at Williams, "let's do high and tights all the way around. You can do me first."

While Williams started the haircuts, Lasher continued.

"Jack here and another soldier, SPC Mariana, will leave tomorrow morning and take my car up to a staging area that we'll be able to walk to after the raid." He looked up over his shoulder to Williams, who nodded that he understood.

"The four of us will focus exclusively on the captives. The DEA has its own mission.

"Thomasito, when we find Maria and Sofia, you get them back to the helicopter. I will stay and walk the rest out to the car. It is about a three-mile walk to the closest road, through a light jungle."

Thomasito looked uncertain. "Jefe, I don't know how to pretend to be a soldier if you don't come back with us."

Lasher thought for a minute. "It's easy. Say yes sir or yes ma'am to anyone that asks you to do anything. Otherwise, don't say anything else. When you land back on Albrook, just walk away with your family. If anyone explicitly questions you, tell them that you report to me and that I gave you specific orders.

"Leo and Julian, you get him back on the chopper and make sure they all get back here. You make sure you get back on the helicopter too.

"Jack, I'll show you on a map I brought where to park the car. I bought a radio set, a good one, from the PX. Once the DEA raid is over, I'll switch over to our radio, and you can talk me in."

Williams was done cutting Lasher's hair. The transformation was significant. Nothing beat a good high and tight haircut.

Thomasito got in the chair next. His hair was not as long as Lasher's had been, but it was unruly.

Lasher continued. "We'll leave here at 4:00 a.m. Once we're on the post, everyone simply does what I tell you to do when I say it. Don't talk to anyone else. If someone corners you, just say yes until you can get away and find me.

"Are there any questions?"

There were none. Lasher spent the rest of the afternoon going over basic handgun safety protocols that every soldier would be expected to know and some basic squad tactics and hand signals. Once all that was over, he told everyone to force themselves to sleep until it was time to go and reinforced with Thomasito's guards that no one was to come in or leave the house until tomorrow afternoon.

By the time all the haircuts were over and everyone had changed into the shirts Lasher bought, they were a pretty convincing-looking crew.

PUGILISM

S harp sat in a luxury skybox, well removed from the crowd. She had two female companions with her, very attractive, looking like runway models or the like. A man sat next to Sharp. He was nearly the exact opposite of her: short, fat, bald, unattractive, dressed in blue sweatpants, a T-shirt, and a pullover cotton windbreaker with a hoodie.

The four watched the boxing ring in the middle of the Atlantic City arena. The undercards were finished, and the main event was around the corner, Mike Tyson vs. Larry Holmes for the Heavyweight Championship of the World.

Sharp was bored already, only present to meet with the potential partner. He was actually interested in the fight, so she had to sit here until the stupid competition was over, waiting to discuss business, wasting so much of her time.

The opportunity, of course, was not in money. She had all the money she would ever need, a near unlimited supply. What she needed were like-minded allies who had pull and resources, who were willing to commit to the cause fully, just like she had. Her people believed that Bill Barber, her guest in the luxury suite, was just such a person. His being here meant that his people felt the same about her.

He had a position similar to hers. He was the benefactor to several Wall Street trading firms. Once she had the infrastructure in place in Panama to move the money undetected, Barber could set up the front side of the operation to integrate her funds into normal market activities, letting the computers harvest and clean it automatically. Then at the right time, switch over to the new market, with a controlling percentage.

Lucky for her, the fight was relatively short, lasting only four rounds, with the contest stopped near the end of the fourth round and Tyson awarded a technical knockout, or TKO.

As the fight ended, Barber relaxed and started the business component of the conversation. "Kimberly," he said.

Her first name used this way was like nails on a chalkboard to her, but this was one of the many prices that must be paid. She had to do her job, and this was it almost entirely.

He continued. "We like the direction you are taking things. I have a half dozen brokerage firms, two with the technology we need. They have made a lot of money in the current market and are desperate to have the same role in the new market. We can pick one or use both. It's up to you."

Sharp processed the information.

While Barber was a disgusting little fat man, the choice of how many hubs got connected in New York was actually very strategic. His bringing her this decision and these capabilities was a big deal. There may not be another benefactor anywhere in the world with this much pull. Maybe the Arabs, but they couldn't deliver the western markets.

Sharp leaned back in her chair, comfortable. "I like the idea of redundancy. We can always centralize on one platform later. I take it then that the other details are acceptable as presented?"

Barber waved a hand dismissively. "Kimberly, you have done a good job keeping the schedule. And you offer a timeline that fits with some of the other strategic initiatives. Your offered terms are fair."

She sensed something. "But?" She wanted to move this along.

Barber made a motion to indicate the other people in the room.

Sharp understood. "Hernando, would you please escort our guests to the club level while Mr. Barber and I finish our conversation? Wait outside the door when you return." She looked at Barber, indicating his man in the room also.

Barber made a dismissive wave, suggesting *you too* to his version of Hernando.

Once everyone left, Barber stood up and paced about, all business now. He even seemed a little taller, in his element.

"Let me get right to it." Barber was serious. "Not me, mind you, but there are a few benefactors on the other side of this—on the demand side, not supply like us—that asked me to vouch for your ability to deliver."

Sharp sat up.

This is terrible news, raced through her mind.

The fact that Barber is telling me means it's early, and I can recover. But the fact that we are here at all could spell trouble.

She stared at Barber, letting him know she was waiting to hear the rest of his statement and that he had her attention.

"Other sources are saying that the entire Panama operation is compromised. I told them if it was, that you would have told us. Better to allow the project to go its course than permit one's ego to get in the way." He looked at her hard.

The weakest of all things is virtue untested in fire. These pencil pushers all work upstream. They don't understand the supply chain, what it takes to run at the very front.

Stay calm.

"Far from it," she said calmly and confidently. "My operation runs at the edge. I have to set up supply lines and build infrastructure in the real world. No one else could have developed this *concept,* not theory. But the whole concept—working, setup, etcetera."

Barber went over to the bar and made himself a drink. He poured Diet Coke into a glass with ice. It looked like he was thinking.

"No one, and I mean no one," he said, taking a sip from the glass, "disputes that this is your vision. You set it up brilliantly. Years ahead of schedule. We will be ready to transition the markets in two or three years. The best alternative didn't have us prepared for two or three decades.

"It's brilliant work, and from top to bottom, everyone knows you are the architect." He walked over and sat at a table so he could look at her straight on. "The word, though, is that the DEA is about to take down the new distribution channel in Panama.

"Between that and news that you are having a problem keeping control of the intelligence assets. Well, a few people on the demand side want me to vouch for you and tell them that you can deliver and that the new supply chain being built is solid."

Sharp went through a few emotions.

She wasn't used to having to answer to anyone or "play politics." She *was* politics. She was who you answered to, not some pencilneck salesman selling the product she invented four layers deep.

"Mr. Barber"—*let's see if I still have some social skills left*—"transitioning the world to a new monetary standard, all at once, with the reveal and technology already in place by the time it becomes public, finding a monetary standard other than the US dollar or a precious metal. It's done. I did it."

Barber drank the rest of his Diet Coke. "So, you are telling me everything is under control?"

"I am telling you that everything is under control. We are on schedule. The technology and product will be in place within the year, and we will have the expanded distribution online."

She emphasized the statement again. "It's done. I did it."

"And you want to use both trading platforms to start. It's twice the expense and logistics, but I agree it is needed for redundancy." Barber leaned forward. "*Since you are on schedule and will deliver on time, no matter what.*" He said the last part in Spanish, Sharp's native language, to emphasize the point.

It wasn't lost on her. She nodded a confident yes, running through the logistics.

No more Miss Nicey Nice, she decided.

"Great!" Barber was back to his unpleasant self, the business side gone. "Now I have a present for you from *your* benefactors."

Her interest was piqued.

She was a god when it came to her projects.

She was a generous benefactor, too; it wasn't all strangulations and torture.

Many of her charges lived beautiful lives, received gifts that would be otherwise impossible in a civilized world. Fulfilled desires that could never be spoken, only experienced. Her benefactors were the same way, and their gifts were always meaningful and enjoyable.

A rush of excitement ran down her spine unexpectedly. A turn from her inner concerns about delivery and schedule, much more than she had let on with Barker.

He saw her interest. "What's your man's name, Hernando?"

She nodded, excited.

"You can have my man if Hernando can take him." He smiled a thin smile at her. "I am heading back. I'll send them in. Good luck, and nice to have you on the team."

With that, he walked to the door, sent the two men in, and closed the door on his way out.

He could hear the faint sounds of a struggle as

he walked away from the door, mingling with the other patrons still exiting the arena.

THE BUS

It was dark out. The bus ride was bumpy. Sofia started out telling herself not to be scared. She was strong. Just stay close to Mom. But they pulled her away. She was now riding with four other children; they were each crying and wailing.

She tried counting; it didn't help.

Tried thinking of her room and her dolls, something happy. But the thought triggered some other emotion. She missed her room; she missed the comfort and warmth of sitting with Dad.

Dad was safe; where was he?

Where did they take Mom? She had looked so scared.

The fear came up from nowhere, suddenly overwhelming her. "*I have to go to the bathroom,*" She told the man in the front seat, not the one driving.

He turned to look at her. "*Go,*" he said with a snicker and turned back around.

That man is mean. I'm a big girl. There is no way I am going to go in my pants.

Another big bump in the road. "*Where is my mom?*" Defiant.

The passenger man turned around again and made some jester with his hand, a circle and a finger. She didn't know what it meant.

The other kids crying subsided; they were watching Sofia. The thought of asking the scary men for things had not occurred to them.

"*My dad is going to beat you up.*" *Maybe they can be scared too. They will see I mean business.*

The man didn't turn around this time, instead snickering, lifting his AK 47 rifle and showing it to her.

I'm going to escape. They can't catch all of us if we all start running.

She looked at the other four kids, three boys and a girl, all about her age, one a little older. They were all scared, turned inwards. None would even make eye contact.

I'll show them how to do it.

Sofia let out a bloodcurdling scream. She dug deep, mustered every tantrum she had ever thrown. It was a loud, piercing wail. She kept it high-pitched, knowing that grownups particularly hated this noise.

Either through understanding or just cold fear, the other kids started mimicking the noise. The bus turned into an annoying echo chamber of children's piercing cries.

The driver slammed on the brakes, irritated by the horrible noises.

The kids stopped as the bus stopped. There was silence when he turned around.

"*I have to go to the bathroom,*" Sofia said, her head held high, proud she had won.

The driver looked at her. He had a meaner look about him than the other man. He stared at Sofia for a while. It was an upsetting gaze, layers to it. Some things she understood, some she didn't.

When he turned around and pushed on the accelerator, Sofia screamed again. When he stopped, and the bus stopped, she stopped.

The driver, calmly, looked at the man in the passenger seat. "*We have an extra, right? Two girls and two boys. We have an extra boy.*"

The passenger man nodded in the affirmative, bored.

One of the boys watched the exchange. He understood what it looked like. He was a little older and a little bigger than the other two.

"*I'll take him. Put her in the seat so she can see out the window.*" The driver motioned to the larger boy and to Sofia. He quickly grabbed the boy by his hair and lifted him up, pulling him out the driver's door, over the seat.

The passenger lifted Sofia up and put her in his lap. He smelled terrible, like sweat and alcohol. Sofia struggled, but he was bigger and stronger than her.

She looked out the front window. The driver threw the boy to the ground. They stood there for a few moments; something was being said, but she could not make out what. Then the driver started beating the boy, hitting him in the head and upper body.

"*No, stop!*" Sofia yelled. The passenger let her rant. She turned her head away. The beating was turning bloody. The passenger turned her head back, making her watch.

She became scared, terrified. The driver was beating the boy to death. She closed her eyes, a hard slap on her head, again, again. She opened her eyes; the slaps stopped. The boy was gone, beaten away.

She grew terrified, cold primal fear. The man holding her was doing something with his pants.

She lost it, suddenly realizing she was in the process of wetting herself. The man holding her stopped, realizing what was happening.

He made a sound and threw her hard into the back, getting her off him. His pants were wet where she had been sitting.

Sofia hit the floor of the bus with the full force of her momentum, losing consciousness.

READY ROOM

It started raining at about two in the morning. Lasher heard the rain hitting the roof of the house. He got everyone up and asked the two sisters to make breakfast for the entire group.

As all that was going on, Lasher shaved.

A soldier was always clean-shaven.

He thought for a moment, taking his shave kit to the kitchen where everyone was milling about.

He handed the shaving kit to Williams. "Go ahead and get cleaned up. Thomasito, Leo, Julian: you need to shave also."

He got funny looks back.

"Soldiers are always clean-shaven," he said, remembering the line from basic training. Both he and Williams smiled. It was an inside joke that anyone who had gone through basic would get.

They left the house at 4:00 a.m. The five people fit well in the big sedan. It would be tight getting all the captives into the car, but there was enough room for it to work.

Better to be safe than comfortable, Lasher thought as he planned ahead for the logistics.

Williams drove the car, and Lasher rode in the passenger's seat. When they got to the Albrook Air Force gate, it was still dark. Lasher used his badge to get everyone through. Since the Panamanians did not have military IDs, they would not have been cleared to enter otherwise. Especially armed, as they were.

They drove to the point Lasher had asked Mariana to meet him at. She was there early, wearing blue jeans and a T-shirt. Williams parked the car. She walked over, everyone except Williams getting out of the vehicle.

She saluted Lasher. He reached over and lowered her arm. "We don't salute in civilian clothes or when in the field. It would give away who the officers are, make it easy if an enemy is observing to know who to pick off."

He handed her a matching shirt. She put it on over her existing T-shirt. Together they unboxed her P226, showing her how to load it, where the safety was, and how to prime it.

He gathered the whole group, standing next to the car window so Williams could hear. "Mariana, you and Williams are going ahead now with the car. Jack, make sure you fill it up with gas before you leave the post."

He gave everyone a radio, headsets for him and the Panamanians, a hand unit for Williams and Mariana.

"We're on channel four. These units scramble the signal, so we won't have our communications intercepted. The batteries are good for about twenty-four hours. Turn them on now, so you don't forget; they have plenty of juice. Their range is about three miles, so Jack, if you can get to the point we discussed, I should have comms with you from the time the raid starts until we meet up."

"That's it. Let's go." Lasher tapped twice on the roof of the car. Mariana got in the passenger seat, and she and Williams drove off.

When the four were alone, Lasher asked, "Is everyone ready?"

Leo and Julian both nodded. They looked nervous but determined.

Thomasito nodded, but he looked terrible.

"Tomas," Lasher said to him, "I know this is tough. You can make it. You can do it."

Thomasito nodded.

"Let's go." Lasher started walking to the hangar that Powers had given him as the staging area.

The hangars ran along the runway facing roughly west. From the runway, you could see Quarry

Heights, the large hill that Lasher had visited earlier. Behind it stood the Panama City skyline.

It had not rained here like it had in the neighborhood, but everything was still wet just from the dew that typically formed overnight this time of year. When the sun came up in a few minutes, it would turn the moisture to steam, creating an otherworldly effect that lasted for about half an hour during each sunrise.

When they got to the hangar, Lasher told the three Panamanians to wait at the entrance. He walked in. There were four AH-6s, the attack version of the Little Bird, in the hangar. Lasher walked past them and through a door that led to an inner area. The DEA agents were all sitting in a ready room right off the entrance.

Lasher stepped into the doorway. "Is one of you SA Hutch?" he asked, formal but polite. It was easy to sound like you were coming in with a challenge. He worked to avoid it.

All the agents were wearing field camo like you would buy to go hunting back home. Many had painted their faces with green and black greasers. A man at the head of the table stood up. He was about as tall as Lasher, slightly above average. The man extended his hand.

"I'm Hutch. You must be Chief Lasher." They shook hands.

When done, Hutch made a blocking gesture bringing his arms up like a boxer protecting his head. "Want to make sure you don't try and take me down like you did, Walker." He stopped the feint move and smiled.

Lasher looked at Hutch. He realized all the DEA agents in the room had an underlying look of defiance as they watched him.

Of course, he thought. *I took down two of their own. Word has spread fast; the tribal drums are beating. I need to diffuse this somehow.*

Lasher adopted an "aw shucks" humble look. "It was my fault; my front walk was frozen, and your two boys didn't see the ice."

Nope.

The looks didn't change. If anything, they became more defiant.

Lasher changed his tactics. "Is this going to be a problem, SA Hutch?"

Hutch relaxed, trying to help the tension leave the room. "Nah, we're just kidding with you."

It's going to be a problem. If something happens out there, I can't count on them backing me up. I don't think they will do anything overtly, but if they can passively not help me, ignore a request for help or something. Odds are they will.

"I have my team outside. Are you going to give the mission briefing from here?" Lasher asked.

"No, we're going to go over everything out there in the hangar in about an hour when the pilots get here. Until then, you're welcome to join us here."

"Thanks. I've got some stuff to go over with my guys. We'll be around, and I'll make sure we're ready for the briefing when you are." Lasher turned and walked out.

He could feel eyes on his back as he left.

KUNG FU

L asher sat with the Panamanians right outside the hangar where he had left them. No one was very talkative. Thomasito looked marginally better the closer he got to the mission starting.

After about thirty minutes, five of the DEA agents walked up to Lasher and his team. It was an aggressive walk with a tall, big man in the lead.

"Hey, kung fu boy," the lead man said, heading straight for Lasher.

Lasher turned and recognized the situation instantly.

These boneheads are willing to go a man down to try and convince themselves they are tough guys. The thought flashed across Lasher's mind. *How many times do I have to go through this same scenario?*

The first time Lasher was confronted by a bully, he got beat up, his mouth writing checks his ten-year-old body could not cash. Grandpa Lasher had not been happy with him losing a fight, even though it was to a group of bigger kids. He was put into an after-school martial arts program the next day, Grandpa attending with him and watching for every session for the next five years.

"You want to do this now? Can't we wait until after the mission?" Lasher said.

The lead man misinterpreted the request as fear. "We don't need you awake, *pendejo.* Your unconscious body strapped into one of the choppers is plenty, *liaison.*"

Lasher knew he would have to put this guy in his place. *It's not going to win me any more points with the DEA,* he thought. *I don't see any other way around this.*

Lasher feinted a punch and stomped his right foot, loud. The big guy flinched, half moving to a fighting position. When he did, he assumed a left-handed posture, not the typical right.

He is no street fighter. He's big and strong, not used to an even fight. And he is left-handed.

The feint by Lasher made the tall guy embarrassed for flinching more than anything else. As quickly as he could recover, he took a swing at Lasher's head. It was a fast move, but he telegraphed it.

He's a boxer, Lasher thought. *He'll be slow but powerful. If he lands a punch, I'll feel it.*

Then his mood darkened. *This is getting in the way*

of the mission. These morons don't take their work seriously.

Lasher had fought all types of people, knowing all kinds of unarmed combat techniques. He used modified Kenpo, or Kempo, as Americans would know it. Having achieved a fifth-degree blackbelt, working over the years to modify the core Kenpo concepts to his preferred fighting styles.

Kenpo focused on both attack and defensive moves. The attacks were primarily power moves, quick and fast, inline to a forward thrust. Not as much grabbing and control, more quick motions designed to end the fight quickly.

He heard Grandpa's voice in his head. *Don't fight to win; fight to end.*

Instead of anything fancy, Lasher moved quickly, striking the man in the chest with a single fast open-handed push, the slightest chance of an actual injury. He caught the guy mid-swing, the force of the impact pushing his attacker backward, taking the wind from him.

I could have hit you a lot harder, even killed you. Please learn from this. We don't have time for this macho stuff.

Lasher quickly went over to the guy on the ground. The other DEA agents half jumped in to stop him, but he put his hands up to assure them he was going to help.

"What's his name?" Lasher said, moving the guy to a sitting position while still gasping for air.

"Deckard," One of the other agents said.

"Deckard, calm down." Lasher leaned Deckard's head forward.

The strike had not damaged anything. Lasher landed the blow precisely, causing the chest and back muscles to spasm, like when you were a kid, and someone gave you a frog punch, only worse. This attack briefly made you feel like your ribs were crushed, the spasms preventing you from getting a good breath even though you could still get air down. It felt like it wasn't enough.

Lasher rubbed his hands together and put one on either side of Deckard's head. He quickly twisted Deckard's head left, then right. It sounded like someone cracking their knuckles. Adjusting the back of the neck sent a signal to the brain to worry about that, not the spasms in the chest, which stopped within a few seconds of the neck adjustment.

Deckard sat there with Lasher right next to him. "Ah," he said with a smile on his face once he recovered. "Got it. Kung Fu it is."

Lasher slapped him on his back, stood, and helped Deckard stand up.

The rites of passage, or whatever this stupid exercise was, seemed over. A lot of the tension left the air.

Deckard looked over to Thomasito and smiled. "You all have to go through this every day in training?"

Thomasito didn't miss a beat. "Yes, sir," he said, just as Lasher had told him to.

Good man, Lasher thought to himself.

THE BRAVES

L asher and his team looked good. Tight haircuts, physically fit, dressed the same. No one
thought about it one way or the other, ac-
cepting his team at face value. The briefing had
been uneventful, going over the same information
Powers gave him yesterday and the same information he had given to Thomasito, Leo, and Julian
yesterday afternoon.

They boarded the gunships around noon and took
off immediately.

The DEA was well equipped. Lasher suspected several of the DEA agents were really CIA. A few of
them stood out as more seasoned. It didn't matter.
They had their mission, he had his.

The AH-6 gunships were graceful. Small, fast,
well-armed. They were light on defenses making
up for it with speed and precision maneuverabil-
ity.

Lasher and his team sat in the back; both sides of

the machine were open air. Lasher showed each Panamanian how to buckle in and checked their harness to make sure they were secure. He showed each person how to unbuckle the belts and had them each do it twice so they could have a little muscle memory if things got intense.

Each Little Bird fired their engines while inside the hangar, drifting out and then up about a hundred feet until all four were in a diamond formation. The noise in the hangar was defending, better once outside but still loud with the open doors.

The four helicopters rose in formation, straight up, then each turned, and together, they headed west by northwest. They would be flying away from the canal into the middle of the country.

Lasher had the headset that Hutch had given him. He could hear the DEA agent's chatter.

The plan was that the gunships would make an initial pass, each firing rockets at the defensive towers protecting the compound and the non-essential buildings like the barracks and ware-houses, then circle the large hill that it backed up to. This was called an offset approach, using a key terrain feature to transition from attack to the landing zone in the middle of a maneuver.

Lasher's helicopter would land right outside the back building that was his target. Since Lasher didn't know what Thomasito's wife looked like, he would have to let Thomasito take the lead once he got them inside the building. He had a picture of the daughter Thomasito had given him. The three DEA helicopters would land on either side of the main villa that Roman used as his house and office. They were doing a smash and grab: secure, land, get in, get the intel, get out.

As they left Albrook airspace, the helicopters stabilized at five thousand feet, about a mile high. The elevation provided a beautiful panoramic view of the military bases, the canal, the Bay of Panama, and the city skyline. Each ship tilted forward and started moving, not overly fast, about sixty miles per hour ground speed. This would put them over the target in just under thirty minutes.

Thomasito was looking better. He was ready to go, finally close to being about to do something instead of feeling useless. Leo and Julian both had their eyes closed tightly. Lasher noticed and pointed them out to Thomasito.

"It's their first time off the ground," he said to Lasher, a slight smile on his otherwise serious face.

The terrain they were flying over slowly changed from city to rural to jungle. A dense canopy of dark green and bright yellow trees on rolling hills. The size of the hills got more pronounced as they got farther into the interior of the country.

After about twenty-five minutes, Lasher felt the AH-6 accelerate, tilting farther forward and starting to drop in elevation.

Hutch came over the headset. "Here we go. Greenlight," his voice crackled in.

"Here we go, fellas. You're going to need to open your eyes."

Lasher had completed air assault training, so he was familiar with the sensation of accelerating and dropping in elevation. It gave you the same feeling as being on a roller coaster when speeding down that first big hill.

The three Panamanians looked uncomfortable. Lasher leaned forward. "Just hold on. It's going to get a lot worse; then we'll be on the ground."

The AH-6s accelerated, even more, reaching about a hundred-fifty mile an hour ground speed. They came in fast, the compound suddenly coming into view. Lasher could feel the machine slow and tilt, the pilot aiming at his ground target. Suddenly, something that sounded like bottle caps went off, immediately followed by a swishing sound as the AH-6 fired two missiles. The first sound was the loader clicking; the second was the propellant igniting, thrusting the projectile forward. The exact sequence happened again, then again.

All the gunships were firing. It was a devastating volley. Almost instantly, the missiles impacted their targets. Explosions went off. Flocks of birds sprang out of the nearby jungle, fleeing the noise. The gunships finished their pass, climbing and turning to their assigned landing zones. Suddenly there was a substantial secondary explosion. The warehouse went up in a massive blast, the heat from it washing over Lasher and his team in the helicopter. The concussion wave pushed the gunship away, causing it to briefly lose stabilization.

"Must have been ordinance in there we didn't know about." Lasher heard Hutch over the DEA radio, followed by the pilots, then team members reporting that they were still okay. Everyone was.

When the noise of the explosion cleared, Lasher leaned in to talk to the three Panamanians. "*Okay, we're going to be landing. Tomas, you're with me. Leo and Julian, all you have to do is get off the bird and use it as cover. Stay by the helicopter door on the side facing the building. Draw your weapons. If anyone that isn't on our team approaches, shoot them. Your job is simply to make sure the bird here stays here until we come out. Got it?*"

They both nodded, nervous but resigned.

"Here we go!" the pilot turned his head and yelled into the back. The sounds of small arms fire started to materialize. With the warehouse going up, the entire compound was covered in smoke, so it was hard to see who was firing or where they were.

The AH-6 came in hard, hitting the ground with a jolt. Lasher unclipped his harness and was off the helicopter in a single move. Thomasito was moving fast, not far behind.

Crouching low, Lasher grabbed his arm and pulled him along, starting to run for the back building. He unholstered his XDM with his other hand. The sound of small arms fire was growing, the DEA would be down also, and assaulting the main villa.

"Stay with me." Lasher put Thomasito's hand on his back to free his. "Hold on, don't get lost."

They made it to the main door, Lasher on the side with the door handle, pushing Thomasito to the other side. He caught Thomasito's gaze and held up his hand to signal three, two...

On one, Lasher pivoted and kicked in the door, instantly rotating back out of the way. After a beat, he swung his head around. There were no walls in the large building, only blankets hanging, creating a pseudo hallway and some private areas. The slight difference between the inside and outside made it hard to see.

Knowing not to waste any time, Lasher went low, running in and along the wall that the door was on. Thomasito followed, moving awkwardly in the crouching stance, but keeping up with Lasher. Handgun shots rang out, hitting the wall well over their heads. Lasher kept moving until he was behind a desk he could use for cover.

He could hear a TV or radio somewhere playing salsa music.

Lasher whispered loudly, "Stay here. Do *not* start shooting. You can't see what you are firing at. If someone finds you, then you can shoot them. Otherwise, just wait here until I call for you. I can clear this place a lot faster by myself than both of us doing it."

Thomasito nodded quickly, understanding. "Thank you," he said.

Lasher gave him a thumbs-up and advanced to another position farther up the wall.

Several more shots rang out. It was starting to sound like there was only one shooter in the building. Whoever it was still fired at Thomasito's position; he had not seen Lasher advance.

Following the sounds of gunfire, Lasher moved through the room. It was a depressing setup, thin mattresses separated by hanging blankets. He worked his way forward toward the gunfire. When he entered one of the small areas, a frightened woman was hiding, staying low. Her eyes grew as big as saucers when she saw him.

Lasher put his finger to his mouth in the universal sign to stay quiet. Once she calmed down, he motioned for her to stay low and head back the way he had come. She did. This repeated itself three more times before he was within sight of the person firing the gun. It was a soldier hiding behind another desk.

Lasher put his XDM away and took out the hunting

knife he bought at the PX. He would be able to get behind the man without being seen. He did just that, grabbed him from behind with his hand over the man's mouth, then inserted the blade up under his armpit, driving it into his heart from the side.

Deep-red blood flowed out. The guard thrashed for a few moments, then was dead, Lasher quietly releasing the body to the ground.

Suddenly a massive explosion rocked the building from the outside, followed by a second blast.

Hutch's voice came blaring in over the radio: "There is a guy with mortars up on the hilltop! Stay where you are. I'm taking one of the AH-6s to deal with him." The high hum of a helicopter taking off reverberated through the building. It sounded like Hutch was sending the chopper Lasher came in to do the work.

It felt like they were running out of time.

Lasher decided to move things along. He started running diagonally to the rest of the areas, finding two more women and no one else. He took them back to the front door, yelling, "Clear!" to Thomasito.

One of the women turned out to be Maria, Thomasito's wife. She was crying in his arms when Lasher got to the door.

"Where are the kids?" Lasher asked, wasting no time.

Maria started to sob deeper. Thomasito answered, "They took them this morning. We just missed them. Now we'll never find her. No one here knows where they went."

Lasher frowned. "I know where they went. The DEA has been observing here for months. How long ago did they leave?"

Maria looked up to answer, forcing her tears back. "They left about two hours ago."

"Okay, that's not so bad." Lasher turned and cracked open the door, then opened it fully. The helicopter they had come in was not the one that took off. It was the source of the explosion, blown apart and smoking. The two pilots, and Thomasito's two friends, had been killed in the surprise blast.

Lasher turned back to the group. "We have to move now. Tomas, take your wife's hand. Maria, take her hand" – pointing to a woman close to her – "and you, her" – everyone understood and held hands with the person in front of them – "Good. Everyone, don't let go. Run as fast as you can when I tell you to."

He couldn't see through the smoke, but he knew where the other choppers would be. There was still sporadic small arms fire, but it sounded far away.

"Tomas, when we start, don't let go, and don't stop. Follow me; I'll get you to a helicopter. Then you get everyone on it, keep saying 'yes sir' until they take off. Then get everyone home to your house. I'll have your daughter back as soon as I can."

Thomasito was in mild shock, his wife and the other women in more profound shock. But they were capable of following his instructions, which was all that mattered right now.

Lasher kicked open the door all the way and started running low. Next to the villa, the nearest gunship would be to his left, not all that far away. The smoke cleared after just a few yards.

Something wasn't right with the DEA. Four of them engaged in a firefight with someone in the villa. They hadn't stormed it yet. This was a huge problem; it meant the element of surprise was gone.

Lasher realized the radio had gone silent too. He kept the group moving, and they made it. The DEA agents were pinned down on the other side of the building.

As Lasher approached, he saw that the backside of the villa had exploded out.

That must have been the second explosion I heard, he thought to himself, piecing together what happened. He kept moving. When he got to the helicopter, he loaded Thomasito and the freed women into the rear cabin. They all barely fit, but it would work. Once in, Lasher tapped the pilot on the shoulder and made a hand gesture for him to take off, which he did.

Lasher watched the gunship ascend and then fly back toward Albrook. With that done, he sprinted around the opposite side of the building so he could approach the four DEA agents. One of the men was Deckard, the guy he had fought earlier. All four looked shell-shocked. It took Lasher a moment to understand why.

When he looked from their position to the side of the building, he saw it. Five DEA agents were down in the rubble near where the door had been. The claymore blast took them out when they kicked in the door.

He looked around and realized he didn't see Hutch anywhere, the agent in charge. Not in the group of DEA here or in the bodies over there.

Lasher turned to Deckard. "Where's Hutch?"

Deckard looked at him, but there was little recognition on his face. Lasher reached over and shook him. "Where's Hutch?"

Deckard's eyes were glazed over, but he was able to focus some. He looked up behind Lasher to the hilltop. One of the AH-6s was up there. Deckard pointed.

Lasher understood Hutch had taken the helicopter to deal with the mortar. "What happened here?" Lasher made a gesture with his head indicating the house.

"We hit some kind of trap." Deckard was back

in the moment. "Set off claymores or something similar."

"What about Roman?"

"He is still in there. We've seen maybe four different guards, but we don't know how many for sure."

Lasher thought for a minute. "Why is the radio out?"

The question surprised Deckard. "I didn't realize it was." He tried a few frequencies. "You're right, it's out. Jammers somehow?"

Lasher decided it didn't matter at the moment. If the radio was out, it was out. "Based on the briefing this morning, we only have about thirty more minutes before reinforcement could arrive." Deckard heard him but didn't show that he registered the comment. The other three agents were not going to be any help either.

I need to get the intel the DEA is after if I am going to get Sofia back, Lasher thought to himself. Grabbing Deckard again, he said, "I'll go in and get him. Cover me. Do you understand?"

Deckard nodded that he heard him, but Lasher didn't think he really understood.

Moving quickly, Lasher ran up to the edge of the back door where the building had blown out. It certainly looked like claymores; the bodies were shredded. If he had to guess, he figured there had been five devices planted around the entrance. He checked each body to see if there was any sign of life, but there was not. Then he grabbed the M16 assault rifle and ammo belt from one of the downed men, as well as two smoke grenades that they had carried.

Lasher thought back to the special tactics urban assault course he had taken. He remembered in the course being impressed with the systematic approach used.

Isolate the building. *Check.*

Supporting fields of fire. *Nope, but I have to hope Deckard can keep his wits about him.*

Tactical movement. *Check.*

Breach. *Well, the back of the building is gone, so check.*

Assault. *Okay, here we go. Move fast, stay low.*

His heart was pounding in his ears. Lasher moved into the villa. It was a large building. The back looked like it had been a laundry room. He moved through it and into a kitchen, staying low with his head on a swivel.

Roman lived nicely out here in the middle of nowhere. The kitchen was well stocked. It had two industrial-sized refrigerators and what looked like a professional stove and oven. Lasher continued moving into the main living area. He saw a flash of movement just in time, taking cover behind one of the large refrigerators just as shots rang out, impacting the big metal machine inches from him.

He tried to swing his head around the corner again to get a better view of the room. Still, rifle fire immediately followed his move, preventing him from getting a complete look.

He changed tactics. *"We only want Roman. If you give him up now, I promise you will live. We are only interested in him. If you make me come over there, all bets are off!"* he shouted in Spanish.

More rifle fire. *Definitely two shooters*, he thought.

He picked up a decently sized piece of drywall on the ground from the explosion. Then he pulled the pin on one of the smoke grenades and threw it where he had seen the movement. He did it again with the other grenade. As soon as he threw the first grenade, there was machine gunfire. Same for the second.

The room filled with thick white smoke and sporadic weapons fire from the men in the room. After they had fired what Lasher counted as most of their ammo, he threw the piece of drywall across the room in the opposite direction of his planned approach.

There was more rapid gunfire until he heard both weapons click empty. He moved as fast as he could, putting the M16 over his shoulder on his back and drawing his XDM. He couldn't see well, but he had a memory for visual images. He knew how the room was organized and where the furniture was.

He advanced carefully, covering the short distance using whatever cover he could. He heard the *click-click* of a new magazine and the primer. They were reloaded. He raised the XDM and fired into the smoke evenly spaced rapid single fire: *Bam! Bam! Bam! Bam!* He fired eight shots in total, just under half the magazine. He heard several shots hit their targets based on the sound a bullet made hitting flesh and the cries of those they hit. He continued running, moving diagonally now, so he was not on the same path as when he fired, ultimately crouching down near a table and reading chair.

He waited, controlling his breathing so it was not audible. His pulse was racing. His body wanted deeper breaths and more oxygen. Nothing happened for several beats. He picked up a book from the table and threw it across the room.

Nothing. Just moaning from the area he shot into.

There's no hurry; wait for the smoke to clear. The DEA guys might be shell-shocked, but they'll keep anyone else from advancing on the building.

He waited for what felt like forever, only about two minutes of real time. The smoke cleared enough in the room to where he could start to make out shapes. There were three bodies on the ground where he had shot. Two were dead. The third one was facedown and doing all the moaning. Lasher cautiously made his way over. He checked the live man for a weapon, then rolled him over.

It was Roman. He was shot in the hand and the stomach. The gut wound was bad. There would be no coming back from it.

Lasher holstered his XDM and drug Roman over to the reading chair, getting him into it and mostly sitting up. He had to shake Roman a few times to get him to focus.

"*Where do you take the children?*" Lasher demanded in Spanish this time, speaking firmly but holding down real anger.

Roman looked at him, not understanding the question but working to focus. Finally, through sheer force of will, Roman responded, "*I need medical help.*" He looked down at his hands, one mangled, both covered in blood, his shirt covered in dark-red blood from his stomach wound.

Lasher sat on the footstool in front of the chair. "I'll get you help; we have a medic outside. *But first, you need to tell me where you take the children.*"

There is no medic outside; it's a lie, but it wouldn't matter. He only has a few moments left, no matter what.

"*I'm thirsty,*" Roman said, regaining some of his polish, trying to command the situation.

"*You're shot in the gut. The blood is dark, and the bullet is still in there.*"

Roman softened. "How long do I have?" he asked, speaking in English.

"Not long."

"I'm really thirsty."

"That's the stomach wound."

They were both silent for a few moments, then Lasher spoke. "I need to know where the children go."

Roman looked at him. "It wasn't my idea. I hate it. But it's business down here, and I am a business-man." He made a head gesture to a desk near a window behind him.

Lasher got up and walked over to it. Nothing jumped out at him. "What am I looking for?"

"Open the ledger."

There was an accounting book in the center of the desk. Lasher opened it; a map fell out. It showed how to get from Yaviza, the end of the highway, to a farm deep in the jungle.

Lasher sat back down in front of Roman. "Where on the farm?"

Roman was sitting up better. He had gone into shock; his lips were gray and his skin tone very pale. "In the main building."

Lasher nodded, leaning in to look closer at Roman. "You don't have too much longer. *Now is your last chance for a confession.*"

Roman started to laugh but immediately coughed up blood instead. "You Soldiers…" He smiled, wiping the blood off his chin with his good arm. "Always thinking that you are in the right. I have no need for a confession. I am doing God's work."

"How is kidnapping children God's work?"

Roman grew angry. "You think I want to? Do you think I woke up one morning and decided I should start pimping six-year-olds? Don't hate the suppliers, my friend; hate the consumer. I have no choice. You American perverts have an insatiable hunger for it."

Lasher was taken aback and a little confused. "I don't understand."

Roman was able to laugh this time. "We supply kids in exchange for the US border patrol looking the other way when we run our product north."

A memory clicked in Lasher. "Is this about some island?"

"Yes."

"Where?"

"Unfold the map. I will show you."

Lasher unfolded the map. Roman pointed to an area just off the coast between Panama and Columbia on the pacific side.

"There is nothing there," Lasher said.

Blood on the map marked where Roman had touched it. "It's there. Can you please get me a glass of water?"

"In a second. What Americans are you talking about?"

Roman spat blood on the ground. "Rich guys. Politicians. Who else would have the pull with the border patrol?"

"Names, Roman. I need names."

Roman told him. Lasher leaned back, stunned.

He could be making all this up, but I believe him. I don't think he would lie on his deathbed. There is no point to it.

"Who else knows?" Lasher asked, recovering a little.

"Who else knows that American politicians fly to South America to have sex with children? How would I know?" Roman was indignant.

Lasher was sickened by the topic. He got up, went to the kitchen, found a glass, and filled it with tap water. When he got back to hand it to Roman, the man had expired. Putting the glass down, he walked back over to the desk, found paper and pen, and traced the map from Yaviza to the farm location, deep in the jungle. He drew the coastline and where Roman said the island was on the second sheet of paper and put both in the pocket of his blue jeans.

The sound of a helicopter landing outside penetrated the villa. A few moments later, Hutch came into the room, leading the other four agents. They were executing a basic cover and move formation. When they saw the bodies and saw Lasher standing at the desk, they stood up and approached more casually.

When Hutch got close, Lasher handed him the map.

Hutch took it. "Did Roman tell you anything?"

"No, he just confirmed what you already knew. This is a map to the farm where they are growing in-country."

Hutch looked at Lasher and the bodies for a few moments, trying to decide something in his head. He seemed to reach a conclusion. "Okay. The price was high for this, but at least we got it. We need to get moving."

There were two helicopters left of the four they came in. As quickly as they could, they collected the downed DEA agents and put their bodies on the floor, three in one gunship and two in the other.

No one was talking, instead focused on the matter at hand. Once everything was loaded, Lasher and Hutch stood outside the helicopter as it warmed up for the trip back.

"I'm not going back with you!" Lasher told Hutch, yelling to be heard over the noise of the helicopter engine. "But I could use a lift to the highway!"

Hutch looked at him. "Chief, if you are going to the

farm in the Darien Gap, understand that we're hitting it tomorrow whether you are back or not."

Lasher looked him in the eye. "There are children there."

Hutch looked down and shook his head. "Look, even if I wanted to give you more time, I don't have any control over when or even if the facility gets attacked. That coordination comes from Washington. It's way above my pay grade."

Lasher pointed to the folded map Hutch had in his hand. "Could you wait to turn in the confirmation?"

Anger flashed behind Hutch's eyes. "I lost five agents today and two pilots. Their sacrifice needs to mean something. There is no way I am holding back the information that they died to collect one second, not to mention one day."

He's right from his perspective, Lasher conceded to himself. *Thomasito lost two friends, and his daughter is still en route to hell.* He wanted to say that but didn't. It wouldn't matter to the DEA at all.

They boarded the helicopter, and it departed, flying due south for a few minutes. The Pan-American highway came into view. Lasher pointed to a turnaround where he could see his car was parked.

Good, at least Williams and Mariana are on schedule and were able to follow my instructions.

The helicopter landed in a clearing about a hundred yards away from the car park. Lasher and Hutch shook hands.

"The whole farm is going up tomorrow around noon," Hutch said as Lasher was exiting. "Save as many as you can."

STORM CLOUDS

L asher hadn't noticed that his shirt was covered in blood. When he got to the car with Williams and Mariana, he had them open the trunk so he could change, putting on an identical shirt he got from the PX. He also grabbed some of the rations he bought, then got in the back seat.

"We have to get to Yaviza. There is a busload of kids that left about three hours ago. They are being taken to the farm," Lasher said.

Williams started the car and maneuvered onto the highway, showing he understood the urgency.

The Pan-American Highway was not what people from the States thought of as an interstate. It was only one lane each way and made from asphalt, not concrete. While there was a posted speed limit of fifty-five miles an hour, there was no enforcement. The vehicle speeds varied between the slow-moving semi-trucks doing about thirty miles per hour and the smaller passenger cars that sometimes did over ninety miles per hour.

"Stop at the gas station in Torti when we get there," Lasher told Williams, who nodded. Torti sat on the border between Panama proper and the Darien province, marking the transition from central Panama to southern. It was about the halfway point of the four-hour drive to Yaviza.

Mariana turned around in her seat. "How did it go?" she asked.

"The DEA bumbled into a claymore trap. Five of the nine were killed. There was a mortar station on the top of the hill that they missed in the pre-mission analysis. It took out one of the UA-60s and both pilots. Two of the Panamanians also.

"They got the intel confirmation they were looking for, and we got several captives out, including Tomas's wife. We lost one helicopter, but it all worked out."

Lasher turned to look out the window, watching the green countryside move by. Then he remembered the island, reaching into his pocket and pulling out the paper where he had drawn its location.

"What's that?" Mariana asked.

Lasher looked up at her. "Homework for you." He handed her the paper. "There is supposed to be an island at that location, but it's not on any maps. When you get back to base, I need you to do some research and see if you can find out anything. Is there really an island there, and if so, why is it uncharted?" Lasher continued to look out the window, letting the beautiful scenery help calm his agitation.

"We're in a time box." Lasher's tone changed back to that of an officer giving a briefing. "The DEA has the location of the grow farm where they are producing Panama Red. They have a squadron of Black Hawks that are going to lay waste to it tomorrow at about noon. It's roughly eight miles east of Yaviza. It's called Yape on the maps I saw.

"There is a bus heading there now with kids. One of them is Sofia, Tomas's kid. This is going to be the last time we know where she is. If I can't catch up to her before they get to Yape, she'll either be killed in the attack or end up on that island you're going to find for me."

Williams stepped on the gas, moving the car down the road as fast as he reasonably could. There was a moment of acceleration, then the constant speed of the vehicle.

Mariana wrinkled her brow, trying to put everything together. "Why would they take her to an uncharted island? That seems odd."

I don't have the stomach to have this conversation again, Lasher thought to himself.

"I'll explain it all later. Jack, go as fast as you can. I am going to try and get some sleep; it's going to be a long night. Wake me when we get to the gas station."

Lasher closed his eyes and was asleep almost instantly, the adrenaline rush of earlier in the day and lack of sleep catching up with him. He felt more tired than he should.

"Grandpa, when you were in the war, were you bad?" Little Dirk asked at the dinner table. Grandpa always made sure they had dinner together. Dirk's friends said they got to eat in front of the TV. That seemed weird to Dirk; he liked the ritual of the evening meal and spending time with Grandpa. He looked forward to it every day.

The big man on the other side of the table looked at Dirk thoughtfully. Grandpa took his naps in the afternoon but always got up in time to make dinner. He was always in a good mood after his naps. They ate at six o'clock every day. Grandpa was a good cook, at least as far as Dirk was concerned, better than the school lunches he had anyway, his only real measuring stick.

Today they were eating macaroni and cheese with hotdogs cut up and mixed in. Dirk thought it was delicious. Grandpa cooked the hotdogs first in a big black frying pan; it made the taste really pop.

"Why do you ask, Diederik?" He put down his fork and looked at Dirk intently, like he was trying to figure something out.

"My teacher said that soldiers are bad, that they kill people for no reason. I told her that you were

a soldier and that you weren't bad, but she got mad at me when I said it. She said that soldiers must be renounced and denounced, but I didn't understand what that meant, and she wouldn't let me ask any more questions. She said I should ask you."

"This is Miss Pasternack?" Grandpa asked, seeming very interested.

"Yes."

"Let's see if we can figure this out together, okay?"

"Okay."

Grandpa pushed his plate away and leaned back. "Diederik, do you think Miss Pasternack is good or bad?"

"I think she is good," Dirk answered, a little unsure. He didn't want to upset Grandpa like he had his teacher.

"Why?" Grandpa Lasher asked. An easy child's question, but the other way around.

Dirk thought for a minute; this was a tricky question. More challenging than he realized. Finally, "I think she is good because she gives me good grades."

"Don't you earn those grades?"

"Yes, of course. We always do my homework right here at the table. I always do everything I am supposed to."

"Do all the children in your class do their home-work and get good marks?"

Dirk laughed. He thought it was funny, "No, Grandpa. Some of the other kids get bad grades. They don't do what they are supposed to."

"If you asked them, would they think Miss Paster-nack was good or bad?"

Whoa! *A light went off for Dirk. This was compli-cated. He had to think for a while, enjoying talk-ing to Grandpa, not wanting it to end where he would have to go outside and play until dark after the meal.*

Eventually, Dirk answered, "I think some of them would say she was bad. But they wouldn't be right. They would only think she was bad because they didn't do their work. Because they didn't pay attention. They would say she was bad because of what they did and how they saw things, not be-cause of her."

Grandpa leaned forward, signaling to Dirk that he was about to say something important. "It's the same thing with being a soldier, Diederik. Some people aren't willing to put in the work a soldier does. They sit back and resent the effort of others. They label them as bad because if they thought they were good, it would mean they would have to look at themselves in a whole different light."

Grandpa paused, looking intently at Dirk. "Do

you understand?"

Dirk thought he did but wanted to ask more questions. But Grandpa was gone. He was calling him from another room. "Dirk, it's time to get up. We're at the gas station."

That didn't make any sense; he wanted to finish the conversation about soldiers.

Lasher snapped awake; Mariana was shaking his shoulder. The car had stopped. They were at the gas station. Lasher could see a colorful sculpture out the window. It was the letters DORIAN about four feet tall, brightly painted with every color imaginable. He got out of the car and went into the small store, heading straight back to where he knew a bathroom was. Once there, he splashed water on his face, examining the wounds from the door fragments he received earlier at the PDF station.

They looked puffy. Redder than they should.

His forehead was hot.

He didn't feel good.

The back of his throat had the telltale tickle of an oncoming cold, which frustrated him.

Those idiots at the PX running the AC so cold. I knew it when I walked in. Suck it up; Sofia is going through a lot more than the beginning of a cold.

It wouldn't be difficult to push past the cold, just frustrating that it was one more thing to deal with.

He stopped at the cashier and bought several candy bars and two cans of Jolt Cola on his way out. Under normal circumstances, Lasher would never put this garbage in his body. Still, he knew he needed the energy and that the next several hours would be exhausting.

He came out of the store with a small paper bag and got in the back seat of the car. It was about 3:00 p.m., which meant they would arrive in Yaviza at about 5:00 p.m., an hour before sunset. If everything worked out as he thought it would, he would catch up to the group with the children right around sundown, sooner if luck was on his side.

Williams finished pumping the gas. Mariana was back in her seat. Once ready, they pulled out, Williams accelerating and driving as fast as he safely could.

"Jack, I don't know if you have been to Yaviza before."

Williams looked at Lasher through the rearview mirror. "Nope. This is as far south as I have ever gone."

"Okay, when we get there, keep going straight through town. It's not very big. Just on the other side on the right is a paved road. Stop there; I'll get out. Then take the turn. It leads to the hospital, the only structure outside of some shanty buildings and huts made from local materials.

"The hospital runs off a generator twenty-four-seven, so it will have electricity. I have never seen any PDF there. If there are PDF, it should be fine. We're rescuing children. They won't know about anything else. They may even help."

Lasher thought for a moment. "Do you have your credentials on you?" Meaning, did Williams have his federal badge?

"No, it's still in my car at the condo."

"Okay, don't worry. Just be big and loud, and use your military ID. There is some office space there for the doctors; you shouldn't have a problem setting up."

Lasher opened a pack of the field rations. He needed to eat good food now, then he would eat the junk food right before they arrived. "We're going to have about an hour of daylight. There is a well-worn trail leading from Yaviza to Yape. It's eight miles. Depending on how many kids they have, they will be moving slow. They may not even have gotten there yet. I should be able to catch up to them while still within radio contact."

The radio system he bought from the PX was a professional system and would cover close to three miles.

Mariana turned around to look at Lasher. "There are rain clouds up ahead."

Lasher looked out the front window. The clouds

were far off, but they were in the direction of Yav-iza.

From nowhere, Lasher coughed.

Williams looked at him in the rearview mirror. Mariana was still looking at him and turned around from the front seat.

"I'm fine," Lasher said, irritated. "I think I'm catching something from the PX air conditioning. They run it so cold on the Air Force bases.

"Once I'm in, give me three hours. Jack, if I'm not back by then, come and get me. But only go to the edge of the radio. We don't both need to get lost, or worse.

"Mariana, you stay in radio contact with Sergeant Williams and me. If we both disappear, wait here as long as you can. The radio batteries are good for twenty-four hours. If no contact by the time the batteries die, head back to Clayton and find Captain Crostino, CO of Bravo Company. Tell her everything that has happened."

Everyone nodded.

"I'm going to try and get some more sleep; wake me when we get close."

THUNDER

The bus filled with thunder, waking Sofia. She rolled on her side then sat up. It was nearly dark out. The road was even bumpier than before. The thunder continued to roll in, sounding scary. The entire experience was just plain terrifying.

She looked at the other kids; they were cried out, quietly sobbing, sitting on the floor.

The man in the passenger seat saw she was awake; he smiled and motioned to the driver. "*Told you,*" he said with a smirk.

Sofia didn't feel good at all. Her head hurt from hitting the bus floor, giving her a bad headache. Her back hurt, and she was very uncomfortable in her wet pants.

She sat there stunned for a bit, not sure what to do but knowing she had to escape. Whatever was going on, wherever Mom was, something terrible was on the other end of this trip.

I don't know what they will do to us, but I know it will be awful if there are more mean men like these wherever we are going.

After a few more minutes, the bus slowed, turned, then stopped.

Passenger Man stood up quickly and turned around. *"Listen, you little bastards. We are going to go for a walk in the jungle. If you get lost, you'll get eaten by a panther. If you run off, you will get eaten by me!"*

It was clear he meant it.

The driver exited the bus and was doing something outside in the under-storage area, where people would put their bags when traveling. He eventually came around to the main door on the other side. Passenger Man opened the door; the driver had a long rope.

No, if they tie me up, I can't get away!

Sofia felt another wave of panic rising. She was now familiar with the feeling of being afraid, but that didn't make it any easier to deal with.

I want to go home!

The driver stepped in; he was bigger than the passenger man, scarier.

"Come here, princess. You're going first," he said, looking at Sofia.

She started to back up, still seated on the floor.

The driver took a step toward her, then stopped, calm. *"Princess, if you make this too hard, you'll get the same treatment as your friend back there, remember?"* He was referring to the boy he had beaten in front of her.

She tried to stop herself from backing up. It was hard. He was so scary, and the thought of getting tied up was terrifying.

The driver stepped forward again. Sofia forced herself not to back away, instead starting to cry again. When he was within reach of her, he grabbed her hair to lift her up. It hurt; she cried harder, snot coming out of her nose and tears down her cheeks.

Suddenly the rope was around her neck, about ten feet free in front of her for the man to hold, more rope behind her; he was now working his way to the next kid, making another loop, then the next. After a few moments, he walked back around to the front and smiled a big smile.

"See, good bitches? If your little rat brains can do it, you better start to learn to do what you are told. Let this be lesson one."

He pulled on the rope, jerking Sofia's head forward. She didn't understand what he wanted; he jerked the rope again. It dug in when he pulled it, burning a little from the friction. He gave it a third pull, very hard this time, forcing Sofia forward.

"When I pull the rope, you walk forward."

He pulled the rope; Sofia still didn't understand. Anger flashed across his face. He slapped her, too hard for an adult to strike a child. She was stunned for a moment, her ears ringing.

"*Let's try it again. When I pull the rope, you walk forward.*"

Sofia was dazed but stumbled forward. He pulled the rope to lead them off the bus. She didn't see the steps and slipped, sliding down awkwardly and landing outside in the mud.

The two men laughed. Passenger Man walked over and lifted her off the ground by her hair. As soon as she was on her feet, hurting badly, the rope was pulled, leading her down a jungle path.

Thunder boomed, and the rain poured down as they disappeared into the darkness.

YAVIZA

L asher got out of the car at the intersection. Williams hit the button to open the trunk. It was raining heavily with no wind, coming down straight and hard. The sun would set in another hour, but the rain clouds made it near dark now.

A painted bus was parked across the street near the entrance to a trail, its main passenger door still open.

Lasher put a jungle hat on from the trunk and rubbed mud on his face from the back of the car. The hat kept most of the water off his face.

He wrapped the ammo belt he took from the raid around his waist and secured the hunting knife in it, opening the end of the hilt to verify there was a compass in it, which there was.

He pulled the radio unit off his waist and put it on the belt, the wire running under his shirt from the belt to the headset.

He checked the load in the M16 and then the load of his XDM 9MM.

Suddenly, out of nowhere, he leaned over and threw up the candy bars and soda. He felt terrible as a wave of nausea washed over him. The rain wasn't helping; he was already soaked to the bone even though he just got out of the car a few minutes ago.

His muscular build was visible under the wet shirt. There was a slight tremor in it from time to time, chills from what was probably a lot worse than just a cold. He could feel his heart beating in his temples, sure he was starting to sweat underneath all the rain.

Trying to focus on the radio, he had difficulty seeing it up close, holding the controller farther away. His eyes weren't exactly right. He couldn't focus. Moving his head around, he could still see fine farther away. Looking back down, he couldn't get the radio to come on, so he walked around to the car window on the driver's side.

"Is your radio on?" Lasher asked Williams.

"Yes."

He fiddled with the central unit clipped to his belt. Nothing. He handed the controller to Williams. "Can you get this to come on?"

Williams looked at him funny, then down to the unit. "It's turned on all right, but it's not working.

It looks broken."

Lasher pulled it off and threw it on the ground. "Give me another one. Check it first." All business.

Mariana leaned into the back seat and pulled a new headset and receiver with a belt clip out of the box. She pulled the contact separator out so the battery would activate, flipped the switch on/off, on/off. The light came on/off, on/off. She handed it to Williams, who passed it to Lasher.

Lasher went through the same routine of attaching it to the ammo belt and running the wire under his shirt. By the time he had it set up, it was wet and didn't work again. He showed Williams, who confirmed; they both made a face of resolution.

"Okay, new plan. We're not going to have comms. Jack, wait five hours, not three. If I'm not back, come get me." He pointed to a trailhead on the other side of the road. "It's not complicated. This is a well-traveled trail. If the map I found was right, just follow it. If it has stopped raining, use the radio. Don't go beyond its range."

He looked at Williams to make the point. "That's an order. Three miles, no more. If you can't find me, go get help. Tell them I made you do all this. Tell them we ordered Mariana; she didn't know any better."

Williams nodded.

Lasher pulled the second radio kit off, threw it to the ground next to the first one, and then turned and ran into the rain and jungle.

It was impossible to track anyone on the trail with the rain, so he just ran, settling into his usual pace. He usually ran six-minute miles but on flat ground, not muddy tree-root-laden jungle trails. He couldn't be positive, but he thought he was making about a ten-minute mile clip through the jungle now; he felt so bad it was hard to tell for sure.

That was too slow; he had to push himself harder. Just because he felt terrible didn't matter. He forced himself to run faster, digging deep. The pounding in his head intensified. He felt the chills more pronounced as they came in waves the longer he ran.

It had started raining even harder. He could only see a few feet in front of him in the fading light and through the heavy downpour.

He was at least two miles in now based on the guess of his speed, twenty minutes or so, not terribly far in a city, but a world away in the dense jungle. The rain was letting up just a little bit, enough to increase his visibility by a few yards. Every now and then, he picked up movement to his left and right. Nothing specific, but it felt like he had a shadow.

How in the world can they move that fast through the

jungle? Am I just seeing things? I hope the fever is not going to start causing hallucinations.

He couldn't run any faster, so instead, he slowed his pace just a little. The shadows also slowed after a moment.

After another ten minutes, he came to a clearing. He would be about three miles in now, not quite halfway to Yape.

He slowed to a walk as he entered the clearing, then stopped. He vomited again, as quietly as he could, hoping the rain would confuse the noise if someone was close by. The exertion and rain seemed to be accelerating the symptoms, whatever they were. The cat scratch itched, and the shrapnel from the PDF station burned.

He was gone for a moment, then realized there were people on the other side of the clearing, maybe a hundred feet away. It was hard to tell visually through the rain, but he could hear voices over the noise of the rainwater hitting the trees and ground. He checked the clearing to either side of him, glancing left then right, wondering if he really had a shadow and if they would show themselves now.

Nothing happened.

Whatever was going on, the talking was getting louder, turning into an argument in a language other than Spanish. He recognized it but couldn't place it.

He moved along the left side of the clearing, staying close to the tree line. It was a roundabout path to take but better than being caught in the open space with no cover. Eventually, he approached the group of people talking on the other side of the clearing. He could see four children with a man in camo on either side of them, two men total. The children were tied together with a rope, the two men yelling at six native Indians, who were blocking the entrance to the path on the other side.

Lasher got close enough to see and hear over the rain, crouching down just on the inside of the jungle edge of the clearing. He felt another wave of nausea but willed it away. He didn't have time to be sick right now.

Then he figured it out. The natives were yelling in Chiriquí, a local language to Central America not based in English or Spanish. They looked to Lasher like Wargandi, an indigenous semi-civilized tribe. It was hard to tell in the rain. The Wargandi were semi-civilized, meaning they were aware of the larger Panamanian society, including the cities and machines like cars, but primarily chose to live away from modernization.

The Chiriquí language was complex, although Lasher could understand it and speak it slowly, with some thought, under normal circumstances. The fever was clouding his ability to concentrate.

What was it? Right. The challenge to Chiriquí is that

it uses a subject-object-verb pattern. In contrast, English and Spanish use a subject-verb-object pattern.

So, in English, something simple such as "I like bananas" would in Chiriquí be "I bananas like." It was harder for the western brain to think quickly in the foreign linguistic pattern in conversation and longer, more complicated thoughts.

The voices turned into a full-on argument. The armed men with the children were speaking Chiriquí quickly, efficiently communicating with the Wargandi. They seemed to be arguing about not following a schedule. Lasher moved closer so he could more clearly hear.

The Wargandi leader was now yelling. *"This was not our agreement! You should not bring children under gunpoint, tied with a rope! Turn away now. You bring dishonor to our lands."*

The men in camo yelled back retorts and brandished their rifles, demanding the Wargandi to step out of the way, which it looked like they had no intention of doing.

They're going to shoot them, Lasher thought. The encounter was escalating out of control. He took the M16 off his back and made sure it was primed with the safety off. He felt a rush of adrenalin immediately followed again by nausea, and then a bad chill hit him.

Push through it. The jungle doesn't care, he thought to himself, finding strength deep down as he always had. *The children don't care. Find the power to do what's right.*

To his surprise, the Wargandi moved first, spears out of the jungle impaling the two armed men. Another six Wargandi warriors emerged from the jungle to issue a second attack close in, killing both men quickly.

Lasher was surprised by the actions. Suddenly there was a noose around his neck. He released the M16 and put both hands on the rope, working on getting his fingers between the snare and his skin. The M16 slapped around, still on his arm with the shoulder strap. The noose was on the end of a pole and whoever had him jerked the stick forward and backward a few times, taking him off his feet and to the ground.

"*I'm here to save the children!*" he yelled as best he could, given the rope around his neck. He managed to get a few of his fingers under it. He tried his best Chiriquí, the speech coming out close to "*children save me,*" which was wrong, then another try, "*me children save.*"

The rope was getting tighter. He reached around to his utility belt, searching for his hunting knife. A hand grabbed him and removed the ammo belt and knife. The leader of the Wargandi, the one who had been yelling at the men in camo, walked over confidently to him as he started to black out, only just able to breathe. Still, the rope was cutting off the blood flow too.

"*I'm here to save the children!*" he yelled again in Chiriquí, then in Spanish, "*Sofia, your father sent me!*"

He saw one of the children swing their head around and look at him just as the Wargandi leader hit him in the face with the back of his spear, knocking him unconscious.

ENLISTMENT DAY

It was Dirk's eighteenth birthday. He had been thinking about this day with great anticipation for as long as he could remember. Today was the slowest school day ever, each class dragging on and on as he tapped his foot, trying to work away the anticipation and feelings of excitement.

After school, he drove himself to the Army recruiters' station to talk to Sergeant Harris. He had been speaking with Harris for the better part of a year, first meeting him when he came to Dirk's small high school to talk about the military as a career. Dirk had all the paperwork and brochures in his school locker. He didn't take them home because he didn't want to argue with Grandpa about his decision.

He signed the papers in the office, and Harris shook his hand. He had chosen 11B as his MOS. Eleven bang bang, he knew it was called; an infantry soldier. There were a few MOSs that offered guaranteed acceptance and a signing bonus. If he signed up for four years, he would get a bonus of ten thousand dollars. If he signed up for six years, fifteen thousand dollars.

He, of course, selected six years.

School would end in about a month. His enlistment would start the following week.

He left the recruiter's office and drove home; Grandpa would be proud. Not thrilled, but proud. He had told Dirk many times that he did not want the soldier's life for him. He thought Dirk could do so much more that he should go to college, maybe law school.

Even Harris, the recruiter, had noted to Dirk that he didn't see too many enlistees for infantry with Dirk's perfect grades.

Harris seemed like a reasonable person, and he had told Dirk almost word for word the same thing that Grandpa had about soldiering, both the good and the bad. Harris had also suggested college to Dirk, then to seek a commission as an officer.

Dirk was having none of it. While he worked hard to get good grades, never receiving anything but an A, he didn't enjoy the process at all and could not imagine paying for four more years of it.

Nope, he was going to be a soldier and help people, just like Grandpa had.

When he got to the house, something was wrong.

There were several police cars out front and tire tracks all over the yard from other vehicles. He parked on the street as the driveway was blocked. The little flat-roof two-bedroom house looked tiny next to all the commotion as he got out of his car and ran to the front porch.

A police officer blocked him from entering. "Hold on there, son," the officer said, putting a hand on Dirk's shoulder.

"I live here. What's going on?"

"Are you Diederik Lasher?"

"Dirk."

"Okay, Dirk. I need you to look at me and calm down."

He did, outwardly.

"When were you home last?"

"This morning before I left for school."

"Did you notice anything strange when you left? Anyone hanging around the neighborhood that was out of place?"

"What? No. What's going on?"

"Has anyone come over recently? Did your father get along with people?"

"Grandfather."

"Okay, did your grandfather get along with people? Did he have any arguments recently that

you know of?"

"No, everything has been fine. Look, tell me what's going on now!"

Dirk could see the front door had been kicked in. At first, he thought maybe the police did it, but that didn't make any sense. He looked into the house, and it was a mess like it had been searched. There was blood on a wall near the kitchen.

The officer moved to stand in front of him again. He could see Dirk was getting mad, so he changed his strategy. "Dirk, several men came to your house around 3 p.m. It looks like they argued with your grandfather; the neighbors heard yelling."

Dirk looked over at the house to his left—the Joneses, an older couple. He cut their lawn from time to time when they were away or couldn't for some reason. Mr. Jones was standing in his yard, talking to another policeman, holding Fritz the dog.

The officer continued. "There was a fight; someone fired some gunshots. Two of them hit your grandfather. We took him to Jackson Memorial Hospital and—"

"How is he?" Dirk interrupted.

Some emotion flashed across the officer's face. He continued ignoring the question for the moment. "When we got here, your grandfather was still awake. There were three dead men. He apparently killed them, defending himself with a kitchen knife."

"What?" Some of this just wasn't registering with Dirk. He wanted to tell Grandpa about joining the Army. Who would break into the house with guns? "I don't understand," he said to the officer. "Normally, I would have been home by three, but today..."

His head hurt badly. He felt sick. There was talking, but he didn't understand it. He was hot and cold at the same time.

He tried to sit up, but someone pushed him back down. When had he laid down? Why was it so cold?

"You down stay. You move no," someone said in Spanish.

SERIOUS

Hernando was on the private jet, flying from Miami to Columbia. Sharp had dispatched him to take matters in hand personally. She had been screaming, showing fear, something he had not seen before from her, on the news of the DEA raid at Los Bravos.

The distribution in Panama was under attack. The timing could not be worse. He was heading to Columbia to enlist Escobar's forces. The Panamanian PDF lacked the required skill to operate at the high level needed to get everything back under control. It wasn't that the PDF were bumbling fools. They weren't, but they were proving no match for whatever these US elements were that were slowly unraveling local operations.

The *Medellín Cartel,* on the other hand, had the necessary expertise.

He would coordinate to send a cartel team in, under the guise of the PDF. If they couldn't finish things, he would have to go himself.

Hernando understood, to a large extent, what the project was.

There were some financial market activities he didn't understand, but he got the gist of it. Crash the US dollar, crash the global gold markets, transition overnight to the new base currency. When the financial markets fall, in the chaos, usurp the major world governments by feeding civil unrest, stoking riots, bringing them down from the inside as world leadership transitions.

It all sounded complicated.

His job was easy: make sure people did what they were told.

He didn't have to figure out what to tell them to do or know how to do it himself. He simply had to provide motivation. Some people responded to violence, others to fear, some others to the possibility of a reward.

He had several hours on the flight, thinking of the best way to utilize the downtime. The private jet had a satellite phone and a laptop computer onboard with satellite access to Sharp's computer server.

Unexpectedly, the phone rang. Hernando thought it could only be Sharp; she was his only contact, and this was her jet.

"Hello," he said as he picked up the receiver.

"Hernando, this is Bill Barber."

Instead of Sharp on the other end, it was Barber, the man they had met in Atlantic City.

"Yes?"

"Are you saying yes, you know it's me, or yes, you are Hernando? It doesn't matter. I have a message for you."

"Yes."

"Uhg. Okay. Hernando, I'm calling to emphasize how important your trip is."

"Yes."

"Hernando. I vouched for you. Well, for Sharp, but you are Sharp right now."

"Mr. Barber. I take my priority only from Miss Sharp."

On the other end, Barber was silent, then, "Hernando, you and I want the same things. I want to keep it that way. Whatever you do, however good you are; do it now, and be it now."

Hernando thought for a few moments. Barber was taking a considerable risk in calling him. How did he even get the number? He wasn't asking for anything, really.

"Mr. Barber."

"Yes?"

"You can count on me."

"Good man," Barber said, and the line went dead.

WARGANDI

L asher opened his eyes. He was in a large building made from trees and grass. The sun was up, and it looked like midday. His clothes were next to him, somehow cleaned and pressed, folded into tight squares. He was under a thatch blanket. He saw Williams and Mariana on the other side of the room. They were sitting at what looked like a picnic table, talking with several children sitting with them. They were doing something on the table. Some kind of game, maybe. He couldn't tell, but their moods seemed high.

The kids were wearing a combination of the clothes he bought at the PX and whatever they had been in when they arrived. They looked clean, and the children looked washed. Everyone looked washed and rested.

He reached over to his clothes and put them on while still under the blanket, noticing his bandages from the PDF station had been redressed using what looked like local plants and leaves. He reached up to his forehead, where it still hurt. There was a large bump. The shrapnel and cat-scratch were dressed but differently, with some native plant under the bandage.

Once he got the clothes on, he sat up, and the blanket fell away.

I don't feel sick anymore. I remember the rain and chasing after the kids in the jungle. Did I find them? I must have. There they are over there. How did Williams and Mariana get here?

"Hello?" he called out. It came out raspy. His throat felt scratchy when he tried to talk.

Williams and Mariana turned their heads at the same time at the sound.

Mariana said, "He's awake," as they got up from the table and walked over.

Lasher started to stand up but found little strength; when Williams saw Lasher move, he hurried his steps. "Hold on, Dirk. Don't get up." He put his hand out to suggest, *Stay in place; don't move.*

Lasher kind of crumpled back down. He was on a bed frame made from twisted grass. "Are those the kids from *Los Bravos?*"

"Yes," Mariana answered, "including Sofia."

"Are we close to Yape? It looks like it is near noon. The DEA helicopters..."

Mariana smiled at him, exchanging a look with Williams. "We're fine. We're not close to Yape. The DEA hit the farm two days ago, on schedule."

Two days? How long was I out? Well, two days, it would seem...

"I'm a little groggy on the details," Lasher said, laying back down, feeling a good, healthy tired.

Both Williams and Mariana pulled stools over so they could sit next to the bed. Williams looked a lot better, too, looking more recovered from beating by the PDF several days ago.

Williams started explaining. "You were lucky you called Sofia's name. After the Wargandi knocked you out, they asked her what her name was, and when she confirmed it, they brought you here to stabilize you and sent a runner to Yaviza, who saw our car parked at the hospital and told us what happened.

"You have been out here for the whole time. They have a medicine woman, of sorts, who patched you up. They used all kinds of plants; I would try and avoid your Army drug test for at least the rest of the week." Williams smiled.

Lasher lifted the bandaging on his arm, and sure enough, there was a foul-smelling green and yellow plant under it, chewed up and spread all over the wounds.

"She said you had an infection," Mariana told him.

"A bad one from the cat scratch and shrapnel from the PDF station, coupled with whatever you caught at the PX. She was amazed you were able to walk, much less run six miles through the jungle."

Lasher sat up again. "Six miles? I only ran for about thirty minutes. That would mean I did six five-minute miles, in the rain and mud, over the uneven trail, while sick as a dog."

"There is some good news." Williams looked relieved when he said it. "The kids that survived are fine. Nothing bad happened to them at *Los Bravos*. They were certainly shaken up, but not abused, or worse." A short pause. "Do you want to meet Sofia? She certainly wants to meet you." Williams was still smiling.

Lasher nodded. Williams stood up and walked over to the table, talking to the children, pointing at Lasher back on the other side of the room. Pretty soon, they were all nodding yes, and they walked over as a group.

As each child said hello, Lasher responded in kind. Their eyes were big when they talked to him like they were meeting a celebrity. After a few minutes, Mariana took them back to the table to their game.

Lasher did learn their names: Sofia, Liam, Mia, and Carlos.

Williams continued after the children left. "I talked to Crostino and explained that we were in hot pursuit of the kids. I told her Mariana was with us. She let Charlie company know."

"Did you tell her about the condo and your capture by the PDF?" Lasher asked.

Williams smiled broader. "Yes, part of it anyway. I figured if you and I were blown, everyone could be. I didn't want to sit on the info that she needed. I told her I recommended calling everyone in until we figure out what is going on."

"Is she going to do it? Call everyone in?"

"I hope so. I was pretty adamant about it. I didn't mention the PDF station, just that they came for me and came for you."

Later in the afternoon, after sleeping for a few more hours, Lasher got out of bed and put on a clean shirt. He was surprised at how good he felt. He was still weak and drained, but there was a warmth and calmness to his inner core he had never experienced before.

He walked outside. The building was in the center of a large village built with similar but smaller structures. He found Williams and Mariana standing outside.

From where they stood, they could see out over the village. The Wargandi were moving about here and there, primarily focused on fishing. There were several men casting nets into the river the village bordered. They wore brightly colored clothing and used a combination of natural tools made from jungle plants and simple modern tools that you might see anywhere.

The nets they used to fish with were hand-made, by twisting hemp into rope through a simple but time-consuming process. They cleaned the fish using fillet knives probably purchased at the American PX. The Wargandi themselves were short and round compared to Americans. Their skin was brown, almost red. Their hair was black.

The building Lasher was in was the largest, built on top of a slight rise. The jungle looked magnificent as a backdrop to the river and village. Broad green leafy plants, tall bongo trees with yellow flowers, green and red bullhorn trees with long pointy hollow thorns. The river was running high from the few final rainstorms as the dry season set in.

The temperature was hot and the humidity high, but neither uncomfortably so.

"How far are we from Yaviza?" Lasher asked as he walked up to the two of them, breathing in the pleasant, flowered jungle air.

Williams turned to answer. "We're about ten miles away, west and north. It's too late to head back today. We can leave first thing in the morning."

Lasher nodded, relaxing. Then the nagging thought hit him.

These kids here are okay, but what about that island?

It sounded like hell on Earth for children.

"We've got a couple different things going on, Jack, Sarah." Lasher addressed both Williams and Mariana. "We have a banking system that is tied to something Noriega and Escobar are scheming. All that work is running through a global organization called Global Bank Group, GBG. Then we have the PDF crackdown on US agents that started on the first day of the new year. The problem with the crackdowns is that it proves someone is on the inside somewhere, and we have no idea who or at what level.

"Those two things, the shadow banking technology and the PDF crackdown, may be related, or they may not be.

"Finally, we have the island Roman told me about off the Panama-Columbian southern coast. I don't know if he was honest, but I can tell you I believed him. He said that they worked a deal with some US politicians. He told me who, but I am keeping that to myself for now. I need to corroborate the information somehow. It's too big an accusation to put in a report until we know the landscape better.

"Each of these is probably bigger than our charter, but together they are for sure. I don't know if I want all this turned over to another agency. If the PDF can crack down on us because someone is feeding them intel from the inside, that's a problem. If the cartels are pimping children to US politicians in exchange for easy border crossings for their narcotic shipments, that's a problem. If Noriega is setting up a high-tech shadow banking system, that's a problem.

"They speak to corruption inside US agencies and a real existential worldwide threat. How do we know that whomever we turn this over to won't be in on it?"

"It's not really up to us," Williams answered.

Lasher thought for a few moments. While he thought, he noticed that Mariana looked like she had something she wanted to say. He looked at her. "Specialist Mariana, does a cat have your tongue?"

She was clearly internally deliberating something. Finally, she made up her mind. "Chief, I want to tell you something that I've kept to myself. I want to tell you, but you have to promise not to let anyone in my company find out."

Lasher and Williams just looked at her, waiting.

Sheepishly she said, "My mother is the deputy director of the DIA."

The DIA, Defense Intelligence Agency, provided foreign military combat information collection and analysis. A little-known sister organization to the CIA, the DIA's mission was more specific than the CIA's mission. The DIA's focus was military information and capabilities. The CIA's focus was much broader, including political and geopolitical matters.

Lasher looked at her. "You're kidding."

Mariana looked genuinely embarrassed. "I don't want anyone to know because I don't want any preferential treatment. I took my father's name. She never changed hers when they got married."

Lasher thought hard. "Could you get me a meeting with her?"

"I don't see why not," Mariana said. "But remember, she is in Washington, D.C."

I must be careful going around my chain of command, Lasher thought. *Are there protocols for this? Yes. Title 10 Code 1034, Whistleblower. I never thought of myself that way, but I can't think of any other safe course of action.*

"I can work with that. I have a couple month's leave saved up. I can go to her as a whistleblower. I have enough firsthand evidence, and I have field evidence," Lasher said.

He didn't like the way it sounded when he heard it out loud, but if this situation didn't fit the whole point of those regulations, nothing did. These were national security concerns, not a local petty disagreement, and he wasn't turning anyone in. He was reaching out for help to close a leak in important military agencies.

Lasher wanted to change the subject. "Do either of you know the history of the Wargandi?"

They both shook their heads no.

"They are direct ancestors of the Olmecs, diverging from the Inca about three thousand years ago. It's interesting. The Olmecs didn't build stone cities like the other cultures. They built stone buildings but used them for arts and science, and probably politics. They lived modestly and worked hard. Massive buildings but modest living. They became expert farmers, artists, mathematicians. Interestingly, they never wrote any of it down."

Williams smiled. "That's good operational security."

Lasher nodded. "That it is. It's also interesting that the Wargandi is one of the few tribes anywhere that held all people equal. Both men and women carry equal status. It's been that way here for several thousand years.

"What is the name of the leader here, do you know?"

"The woman who has been nursing you is called Ava," Mariana said. "She seems to run the place. The guy who was the leader of the war party that brought you here is called Mateo. But we haven't seen him around, except when we first arrived. I think he and his group spend a lot of time patrolling away from the village."

Right on cue, Ava came walking up to the small group from the center of camp.

"*I see you are feeling well enough to stand. That is good news,*" she said to Lasher in perfect Spanish.

Lasher nodded. "*I am. From what I am told, I owe my quick recovery to you. Thank you and thank you for your hospitality.*"

She waved a hand dismissively. "*You have a strong body and pure spirit. It made my work that much easier.*"

They talked for a while longer, Ava letting them know that the tribe would be putting on a "welcoming dinner" tonight now that Lasher was awake. Eventually, she left.

Lasher went back inside and took another nap.

Later in the evening, there was a big fire burning in the center of the village. The scene reminded Lasher of a Hawaiian luau. He, Williams, and Mariana sat on the ground. The four children sat next to them. There was plenty of food, including fresh-caught fish and a variety of cooked vegetables and local fruits.

While they ate, the Wargandi put on a show, dancing in front of the fire, telling the tribe's creation story. The villagers chanted and sang, creating a musical rhythm for the storytellers. It seemed the Wargandi were born from a jaguar impregnated by the jungle itself. The jaguar god brought mathematics and farming, teaching the Wargandi how to use the stars to know when to plant and harvest.

The jaguar god introduced them to the Olmecs, the rubber people, the builders from the before times. The Olmecs built large buildings near here, showed the Wargandi how to keep them secret. Taught virtue, live small, and work big. Gave the Wargandi a magic drum to could use in war, which they did, often.

There was eventually some political intrigue around tribe leadership. Ultimately, the location of the drum and the buildings was lost in a flood.

As a special treat for Lasher, they acted out him trying to save the children from the camo men and the Wargandi coming in and saving the day at the end of the story. The whole village laughed when they acted out getting Lasher in the noose, him flailing about, being jerked around. They made it a good-natured comedy at the end with him getting knocked out; apparently, the funniest thing they had seen in some time based upon the laughter.

As the evening was winding down, it started to rain again, forcing an early end to the festivities. It eventually rained so hard that the rain put the fire out.

Once back in the large building, Lasher sat at the picnic table along with the four children, Williams, and Mariana.

"Get everything packed up," Lasher said to the group. "Let's plan on heading out at first daylight. Ava is going to give us a guide. She said it is about a five-hour walk from here."

Everyone nodded. The noise from the rain outside hitting the thatch roof created a soft backdrop of pleasant noise.

There started to be popping sounds underneath the noise of the rain. At first, it was indistinguishable from the rain, but the pops grew more pronounced. Everyone realized it was gunfire at the same moment, looking at each other with that far-off, wide-eyed look that said you were waiting to hear it again to confirm it.

Lasher and Williams jump off the bench simultaneously, Lasher running to his pile of equipment near his cot, Williams to his on the opposite wall.

"Mariana, get the children and get them out the back. Hide with them at the jungle's edge. Go!" Lasher yelled.

Mariana did just that; the kids were suddenly afraid but not crying. She had them hold hands and then ran out the side of the building, facing away from the main village.

Lasher slapped on his ammo belt as fast as he could, grabbing and holstering his XDM, grabbing the M16, and putting on his jungle hat. By the time he was done, fast as he was, Williams was over next to him, having much less gear—just a jungle hat and his P226 9MM handgun—and pushing over the few torches lighting the interior of the building, leaving it now dark both inside and outside.

The gunfire became steady. It was impossible to identify unique weapons, but it sounded like six or seven shooters total.

Lasher looked at Williams. "Are they shooting the villagers?"

Williams gave a return shrug that said *I don't know, probably,* and *what else could they be shooting at?* all at the same time with the simple gesture.

"Follow me," Lasher said, heading out the back of the building and around the side so they could get to the center of the village without someone seeing them come out the front, where they would have been an easy target.

Muzzle flashes, hidden partially by the heavy rain, made it look like there were two teams of men, three per team, moving from structure to structure, shooting into it. Any villager who left their cover and ran was also shot. It was a bloodbath of the worst kind, gunning down unarmed people who were peaceful and sleeping.

"They are going to murder everyone in the whole place," Williams said quietly as they moved forward, keeping to the shadows.

I see two teams. They look like PDF. Would they have more in reserve? It doesn't matter. If we don't act now, they are going to kill everyone.

Lasher gave Williams the hand signal for charge,

twitching his hand forward twice as he started to run. He had the M16 drawn and was advancing at a run with his head on the sight, elbows in, safety off. The two teams of PDF were working opposite sides of the dirt path between most of the huts.

Lasher signaled for Williams to take the team on the opposite side. Williams sprinted to the other side of the path and disappeared into the darkness. He didn't have a lot of time but wanted to wait for Williams to be in position. Suddenly more shots rang out in a different pattern. It was Williams emptying his P226 into the second PDF group.

Quickly flipping the fire control to semiautomatic, he pulled the trigger. Three round bursts slammed into the three PDF soldiers on his side of the path. They had been busy preparing to fire into another grass hut. He pulled the trigger three times, aimed once at each man, nine shots total in under a second.

Lasher stayed low, not knowing if other teams were watching and waiting for a counterattack. Suddenly over the rain, the sound of a helicopter rang through, followed quickly by the swoosh of missile fire. The building they had been staying in behind them exploded from the impact of some type of rocket.

He couldn't see the helicopter, but he could hear it; it was close by. Machine gunfire rang out, impacting into the center of the village. It was either an

M60 or M240. Probably an M240 based on its accelerated rate of fire.

The PDF doesn't have M240s, Lasher realized. Little good it would do now, but he put the thought away for later.

Instinctively, he and Williams were running toward the jungle line. The machine gun was using tracers. They could see that it was not targeting them, instead hitting the buildings that the ground troops didn't get to.

Several more missiles slammed into the area, the helicopter was saturation bombing the village.

Lasher and Williams continued to make their way through the jungle, circling back around to about where they thought Mariana and the children would be. The helicopter continued to rain destruction down. At this rate, the entire village would be destroyed with little sign it ever existed.

They could hear the sound of children crying and came upon Mariana and the group. Mariana looked nervous and had been crying herself, but she did a good job staying in control and keeping all four children with her. Turning to see the destruction, the helicopter was now visible and making its way to land in the middle of the buildings, roughly where the party had been an hour ago. Two men came up to greet the machine, two more getting off. A heated discussion took place, then one of the men pointed in the direction of Lasher's group.

All four were dressed in dark jungle combat clothes. If they had been US soldiers, they would have been special forces. They had that look.

Lasher took his hunting knife off his belt and handed it to Mariana. "There is a compass in the hilt. We need to go southwest. Jack, you carry two kids. I'll carry two. Mariana, you take point. Watch the compass and keep us heading south and west."

Lasher picked up Sofia and one of the boys, Williams taking the other two. Mariana oriented the compass, and the group turned, heading into the rain-soaked black jungle.

JUNGLE

The jungle was very dense. It might take a minute or two just to take a step, looking for open ground, moving plants out of the way. Every plant out there ended up rubbing against you, be it your hand, arms, neck, or face. Mariana could feel a spot on her neck that was starting to burn. Probably some type of poisonous plant, like poison ivy or poison oak.

She had scratches on her arms. There was some pointy plant here and there with little thorns. They got in your skin then hurt when rubbed one way but not the other.

She was nearing her breaking point.

Her neck hurt, and the water ran the irritation down her back, spreading whatever it was. She couldn't tell, but it felt like someone was watching her too. She had that feeling of being followed. It was hard to see the compass between the pitch-black night and rain. It was a cheap compass; it sometimes provided an incorrect reading if she didn't hold it steady and level.

The rain created a constant background noise.

I was initially happy for the chance at fieldwork! She laughed to herself, trying to keep her spirits up. She had debilitating fear at the edges, getting close to being overwhelmed a few times, using her inner resolve to pull herself back.

She was a good soldier, though. Tough. Basic training had presented enough experiences that she could draw upon.

She looked back. Lasher and Williams were each carrying two of the children. They looked like a family on vacation, each parent with a child on either shoulder. *They have it tougher than me. I must keep going,* pushing forward through the fear and into the night.

After a couple hours, movement got even more challenging. Lasher wasn't sure how far they had gone in the past two hours; he didn't think it could be more than a mile, maybe a mile and a half.

The rain had subsided into a drizzle. They got just as wet but could hear better.

"We're leaving a heck of a trail," Lasher said, stopping, turning to Williams. They were both still carrying two kids each.

Williams put his two passengers down; Lasher did the same.

Looking at his watch, Williams said, "It's just after

1:00 a.m."

Mariana walked back from the lead into the group. "We've been going more west than southwest. It's the best I could do given the terrain."

Lasher nodded and looked at the four children. *"Do you think you can walk for a while with us?"*

They each nodded that they could, looking spooked but very alert. Lasher gave them a thumbs-up. They each returned the gesture, Sofia using her opposite hand to hold her finger in position.

Williams had an uncomfortable look on his face. "This is insane, Chief. There is no way the PDF attacked that village. I know I saw it, but it can't happen. It makes no sense. They just killed forty people. That's mass murder."

We've just triple confirmed there is a mole somewhere in Bravo Company. The information is feeding all the way up the chain, maybe all the way to Noriega. Someone high enough to order the murder of dozens of Panamanians is on the receiving side of this information. There must be something we know, or that they think we know, that has them terrified about its disclosure. These are over-the-top overt methods to come after us. What could be worth the lives of all these innocent people?

"There is something we know that they don't want to get out. It's either the banking technology or knowledge of the island," Lasher said.

I need to take control of this situation, he thought as he looked around. *I have four scared and crying kids, a scared and crying specialist, and both Williams and I are nowhere near one hundred percent.*

On top of that, we have trained killers hunting us in the jungle who were tipped off to our location through an internal mole. How did things devolve so quickly into this mess?

"Jack, I assume you told Crostino about the village?"

Williams looked at him, surprised. "Yes. Are you accusing me—"

Lasher cut him off. "No, and I'm not accusing her either. I just know how she operates, and I don't believe she could be the mole. Is there anything else you can think of that happened during your phone call with her?"

Williams looked down, replaying the conversation in his head. "It was a pretty standard conversation. She did legitimately seem surprised about our situation. I know she took some notes. She assigned Cruz to work tactically on her end. Said she would coordinate with Charlie Company about Mariana."

"Cruz? Was he on the phone with you?"

"No, my impression was that he was in the room, but not that he was on the line or that I was on speakerphone or anything."

"It's Cruz," Lasher said, a matter of fact, working everything through.

"You can't possibly know that." Williams was immediately in denial.

"I know. He knew where you were on Gumball. He knew where I was on Raincloud. I'll be honest, I don't know if he is intentionally selling us out or if he is being run. When I picked him up a couple nights ago, he had a woman at his house. I didn't see her, but she called out in Portuguese to him. He might just be running his mouth to her, and she is the spy.

"Either way, it's Cruz. He might not be the mole, but he is the hole."

Williams looked skeptical. The conversation was cut short when there was the sound of a stick breaking a few dozen yards back the way they had come. Both Lasher and Williams heard it and glanced in the general direction.

I don't see how anyone could be tracking us in this storm in the dead of night, but I can't take any chances.

"Mariana, retake point," Lasher said, shifting his focus. "We have to get moving. Find an animal trail and follow it. Try not to leave any marks. We need to get to a place we can regroup, and we're not going to do it cutting through the jungle this way. We're practically leaving a 'they went this way' sign in our wake."

Turning to Williams, he said, "Jack, you are in charge of the kids. I don't know how much gas they are going to have or how far they will be able to walk." He lowered his voice. "I am going to hang back and see if we are being followed. Have Mariana lead, the kids hold hands, you in the back of the line to make sure one doesn't wander off or get lost."

He walked over to Mariana. "Let me see the compass."

She handed the hunting knife to him. He got his fingers around the small compass in the hilt and pried it out, keeping the blade and handing the compass back to her.

"I might need the knife," he said to her.

She nodded, understanding, but wished that she didn't.

She looked at Lasher. "I think something is following us."

"Something, or someone?"

"Something. I keep catching glimpses out of the corner of my eye, something big, moving low, always just out of sight."

"Okay, stay alert."

Mariana nodded and moved ahead in the dark and rain as Lasher disappeared back the way they had come. She had the small compass in one hand and was holding Sofia's hand with the other. Each child held hands. Williams walked in the back a few feet behind the last kid.

After another two hours, she finally came across a game trail. It was running roughly north and south. As she cleared the jungle, she looked in both directions along the trail, stepping far enough in so that the four children and Williams could clear the jungle also.

"Sergeant," she said to Williams, "do you want to head left or right? Left is south."

Before he could answer, there was a flash of movement across the path, then a low guttural growling sound. Mariana screamed; Williams pulled the children over and behind him, crouching down and looking in the direction of the noise.

Mariana let go of Sofia's hand as Williams pulled the child away. She quickly put the compass in her pocket and drew her P226.

Suddenly from nowhere, a big black cat, a full-grown panther, leaped on her. It was a massive animal at two hundred pounds, maybe more. She was quick enough to fire at it, hitting it twice, but the cat was on her, biting her upper shoulder, ripping her back with its claws. She screamed a primal sound of both pain and terror, harrowing and full of fear and distress.

As fast as he could, Williams fired into the large animal, the children near him putting their hands over their ears from the loud report of the handgun. After the tenth round, the cat collapsed but was still on top of Mariana.

The children all began screaming and wailing in pure terror, besides themselves with fear, immobilized with fright.

Williams got up and tried to move the cat off Mariana. It was challenging, but he was able to eventually push it to the side.

Mariana was still alive but was torn up badly. Dark-red blood flowed from her shoulder. It was a high wound. There would be no way to apply a tourniquet to it. She was in shock, trying to talk but just stuttering. Her breathing was labored. The bite may have punctured her lung as well.

Lasher burst through the jungle entering the game trail a few dozen yards to the south, seeing the dead cat and Williams tending to Mariana.

"Oh no!" he said, running over and dropping to his knees by her, on the other side from Williams, who held one of her hands. Lasher took the other.

"You're going to be okay, Sarah," he said, knowing it was a lie.

She was trying to say something but couldn't get past the first syllable, instead repeating, "T-T-T-T."

There was blood under her on the jungle floor as well. It was just as dark as the shoulder wound.

After a few more moments, she expired, slumping down. Both Lasher and Williams watched the light fade from her eyes.

The four children were wailing in an absolute panic.

After a while, the kids stopped screaming and settled into sobbing. Lasher and Williams sat holding Mariana's hands for longer than they should have. Everyone was in shock.

I owe Mariana a debt I can never repay, Lasher thought to himself, working to hold on and not become depressed. He looked over, and Williams had tears mixing with the rain as he sat there. It wasn't just that Mariana had been killed, but that both Lasher and Williams felt a deep sense of responsibility for her, for bringing her along in the first place.

Suddenly reality snapped back in, the noise of the rain coming from nowhere. *Our pursuers are going to have heard all this noise.* Lasher heard himself thinking, then realized what it meant.

"Jack," he said.

Williams looked up at him, struggling to stay in control.

Lasher, standing up, handed Williams the M16. "They're going to know where we are now," he said to Williams, whose expression suggested he didn't understand, as he was still in shock.

Lasher pushed the M16 into his hands. "They are going to know where we are now," he said again.

This time Williams understood. "What are you going to do?"

Lasher looked back the way they had come. "Get the kids into the jungle on the other side of the trail. Just a few feet. If you see anyone that isn't me, shoot 'em. I am going to circle around. I imagine the PDF are moving this way as fast as they can. I'll ambush them and take out as many as I can. Open fire when you think the time is right."

Williams nodded, spun to the children, and moved everyone to the other side of the game trail.

Lasher stayed low and ran back to where he had entered the trail, then turned and disappeared into the jungle. He didn't go very far off the game trail, needing to stay close and maintain a line of sight, limited as it was with the rain. The wails of the children subsided.

Good for Williams. He got them to calm down.

It started raining harder.

There was no sound except the sound of rain.

Nothing happened for quite some time. Then, underneath the noise of the rain, the sound of movement filled the area. Moving slowly and carefully, two men emerged on the edge of the trail. They were the same men Lasher saw get out of the helicopter.

There are two. Where are the other two?

They stopped and crouched down, a few yards

apart. Looking left then right. They saw the large, dead, black cat and Mariana's body. One signaled to the other, who carefully walked over to examine both. After just a moment, he made a hand signal to the other man, sliding his hand across his throat, indicating that Mariana was dead.

For some reason, the gesture infuriated Lasher. He felt a rise of anger and frustration.

These men just murdered an entire village and got Mariana killed! Stay calm. Wait as long as you can. Either the remaining two will show up, or these two will get close enough to Williams where I have to act.

The man who examined Mariana stood up, looking all around, listening. He seemed to have decided the area was clear, motioning back into the jungle.

The two other men Lasher had seen emerged from halfway between his location and Williams.

I'm glad I waited. They would have had me dead to rights in a crossfire.

But it was now Lasher and Williams who had the four men in a crossfire.

Lasher opened up with his XDM, leaving his cover and charging forward, gun raised, elbows in, even spacing between rounds. Williams started firing a moment later with the M16.

It was over nearly before it started. The four PDF soldiers were shot down too quickly for them to react.

Williams emerged from the jungle and started searching the downed men. Lasher continued past him to the children and ended up in an unintended group hug.

HOSPITAL

The group moved down the game trail as far as possible, heading south until the path turned west. They stopped there.

"What time is it?" Lasher asked Williams. Lasher did not have a watch. Williams did.

"It's almost 5 a.m.," Williams said, putting down the two kids he was carrying. Williams had taken turns carrying two children while the other two walked.

Lasher put down Mariana's body.

"I'm sorry I got you into this," Lasher said, looking down the trail at the turn.

Williams smiled. "You rescued me from the PDF station. I would say this is better than that."

I had completely forgotten about that. I am getting tired, Lasher thought.

"How close to Yaviza do you think we are?" Williams continued.

"I think we're close." Lasher sat down, exhausted. "I can't get the jungle training out of my head. SURVIVE was their stupid acronym. I can't remember what it stood for."

Williams also relaxed. "Got me. I never took the course."

"They made us drink blood from a boa constrictor."

"Did you do it?"

"Sure, what was I going to do, fail the course after two weeks of misery?"

"They waited 'til the end, huh?"

"They always wait until the end," Lasher said, reflecting on the experience. "The sun will be up in about ninety minutes. Let's rest here until then. I'll take the first watch. Try and get some sleep. The kids need some sleep also. I'll wake you up in an hour."

Williams nodded, motioned to the four children to come closer. They all laid down in the mud together and were asleep almost instantly.

Lasher kept watch, mostly listening for any noise. It was still raining, but only just as much a mist now as anything.

Nothing happened. After an hour, he woke Williams up, careful not to disturb any of the sleeping children. Williams got up, and Lasher laid down. He was asleep as soon as he allowed himself to relax, almost instantly.

As soon as he closed his eyes, he heard shouting and snapped them back open. The sun was up. He had been asleep for at least an hour, maybe two. Williams was yelling at someone or something. The noise woke Lasher and the four kids.

Lasher looked around; Williams was yelling at him from up the game trail. It took Lasher a moment to get his wits. Mateo and several Wargandi, the same twelve he had first encountered in the clearing, were walking with Williams.

"Look who I found," Williams said, looking happy and pointing to the trailing Wargandi warriors.

When Mateo walked up, he made the noose motion and a gurgling sound, pointing at Lasher, waving his arms. Smiling a sad smile.

"Mateo," Lasher said, standing up, doing his best to get his head together after the short sleep.

"Lasher," Mateo said, transitioning from his silly gesture to seriousness.

"*I am sorry we could not save your village.*"

Mateo looked at Mariana, crumpled and bloody on the ground. "*We all lost. You tried to help us. We tried to help you. We could see you fight back. You did well. The black machine was the devil. Too powerful for you. Too powerful for us. But we live in Panama. We are used to pain and tragedy.*"

"*What will you do now?*"

"Same as we do every day. There are many of us the black machine did not kill, more than you may think. We will honor the dead by placing them with their ancestors. We have a sacred area in the land for that. What will you do now?"

Lasher looked down at Mariana's body. *"Same as you, I guess. Do what I always do. Take Mariana to be placed with her ancestors. Then I will find whoever was behind the black machine, who sent it, and I will introduce them to their ancestors. For all of us."*

"Would you like us to show you the way back to Yaviza?"

"Please, yes."

Lasher picked up Mariana's body; a Wargandi picked up each of the children. When everyone was ready, they headed off the game path, following Mateo. The Wargandi knew how to move through the jungle. This was their natural habitat. The going was easier in daylight as well. After an hour, the group emerged up the road from the Yaviza hospital building. Lasher indicated to it by pointing, and the Wargandi carried the four children right to its main door entrance.

The hospital building was of modest construction, probably built within the past fifty years, after the digging of the canal, but not so recently that it looked modern. The Wargandi seemed otherworldly in its parking lot and against its main entrance.

Lasher and Williams shook hands with Mateo and each of the Wargandi men, who disappeared into the jungle so seamlessly they just seemed to fade away.

A Panamanian nurse came out the door with a bed on wheels, hurrying to Lasher, who still carried Mariana's bloody corpse, not realizing that the time for medicine had come and gone.

A few more nurses came out. Lasher watched them, not really registering what was going on. He realized that he was in shock, the death of Mariana and the jungle ordeal, plus everything else, catching up to him.

If I am feeling this, I can't imagine what the poor kids, and even Williams, are going through.

Before he knew it, the nurses had him and Williams in wheelchairs and walked the kids back into the emergency room. They ended up giving each child a mild sedative, and all six of them ended up in hospital beds in a shared space, everyone getting an IV to restore fluids.

Lasher called Captain Crostino and filled her in, asking her not to let anyone else, including Cruz, know where he and Williams were. He told her about Mariana and got the number for the Charlie Company CO, who he called next.

Accidental deaths were covered under Army Regulation 638-8. The regulation held the procedures for notifying the soldier's family, mortuary affairs, and benefits if the soldier had a surviving family. Lasher worked it out with the Charlie Company CO, having the CO notify the family but documenting Lasher as her direct supervisor at the time of death. Lasher would accompany the body home and represent the unit at the funeral.

When he was finished on the phone, he looked over to Williams, who was asleep. Everyone was asleep. As he allowed himself to drift off, he kept having nagging thoughts about the island. The idea of the island and unpleasant thoughts about what was going on there would simply not leave his mind.

RETURN

They all slept the rest of the day and night, leaving the hospital after a good breakfast the following morning. Lasher filled out the paperwork, and the entire stay was billed to his field operations account. Mariana's body would be sent to Rockville, Maryland, the funeral to be held in four days.

Lasher would accompany the body and represent the Army at the funeral, along with a small honor guard, two soldiers, the complement that the regulations allowed for lower-ranking enlisted. They would be local, doing a detail. Lasher would be the person that knew Mariana and who was responsible for her accident.

The hospital had a small sundry store. He bought some snacks and drinks for the ride back on the way out.

They loaded the car and pulled away, Williams driving and Lasher in the passenger seat, the children sleepy again and all four in the back seat, a pile of drowsy exhaustion. It took a few minutes to navigate out of the town. There were only two roads, but they were dirt, so it was slow going. Once past the town, the road changed to pavement, and Williams accelerated. Not as fast as the drive here, a good but safe speed for the return trip instead.

"Where are we going, other than back to the city?" Williams said after a while.

It was a clear day, and the sun was bright. There was a good feeling to it. It felt fresh after the rain, cool and pleasant. The rain worked the humidity out of the air and made everything feel new.

"First stop is to get Sofia back to her house. We'll let Tomas find the other kids' parents. As you mentioned, the Army isn't in the business of worrying about lost Panamanian children."

Williams looked over to Lasher. "Dirk, that's not what I meant…"

Lasher wasn't angry; he had done a lot of thinking. "Jack, you were right. I was wrong. I'm not saying we should have done nothing. We had to do what we did, but we didn't do it as US Army soldiers. You were right. This wasn't part of our charter."

Williams was not used to Lasher thinking like this. "I never meant to suggest we shouldn't save the kids. I'm glad we did. It felt like the right thing then and still does now. We paid a heavy price, but Mariana would agree, it was the right thing to do.

I bet she would make the same choice, to do it all again, even knowing the price."

Lasher was quiet for a bit, then, "It was the right thing to do, and yes, the price was too high. It always is. We do it anyway. Still, you were right. Our job as agents is to collect low-level information and report it. The Army brass tells us what information they want, not why. The why doesn't matter to the job.

"It's a big machine. Analysts like Mariana, God rest her soul, organize what we report. They probably don't even really know the why's. Who knows what happens next.

"Anyway, you were right, and I was wrong. I have spent a decade chasing a rainbow that doesn't exist." Lasher looked out the window. "I joined, I think, to impress my grandpa, who raised me. I never told you this, but he actually died the day I enlisted—before I could tell him. He never knew I joined up. I've been trying to impress his ghost, I guess.

"Chasing rank. Jack, do you have any idea what it took to make W3 with only ten years in service?"

Williams shook his head. He really didn't, but he did know it was near impossible. "I watched you do it. You had a lot more energy than I did."

"Maybe." Lasher thought about it. He had been burning the candle at both ends for too long.

As he sat in the car, he was tired. More than just the past couple of days tired. Maybe it was the drugs from the plants the Wargandi used, but he felt like his head had cleared—fully cleared—so he could really think for the first time in a long time. He was physically tired, but he felt like his core was whole again and healing, using his body's energy to get better. He didn't realize it until now. Having it all back made the difference. He was experiencing an inner peace he had not known before.

Lasher looked back over to Williams. "I'm done."

Williams made a face, not taking his eyes off the road. "What do you mean you're done?"

"I'm done. I am going to resign from my commission. I'm out."

"Can you even do that? Don't you have a service obligation?"

"It's up next month. Five years from my warrant. I didn't have to renew it for W3 because I got it so close to the original date."

Williams took his eyes off the road and looked at Lasher, trying to see if he was serious. "You're halfway to retirement. Even if you never get another promotion, you'll have enough retirement to live however you want. You're halfway there," he emphasized again. "You make what an O3 makes. That's good money, more than a civilian job."

Lasher smiled; he had gone through all of this yesterday as everyone else slept in the hospital. "The Army can't get me what I am looking for. Maybe nothing can, I don't know. I want to help people, Jack. I have a good set of skills. Better than most.

"When I was growing up, I heard stories about WW2, how the soldiers would liberate villages, save people from the German occupation. That's not the mission anymore. It's a big machine now. You know that. You told me that just a couple days ago. I didn't understand then. I still had my rose-colored glasses on. I thought if I could just get the right rank and the right assignment, that it was still out there.

"To find what I am looking for, I have to start looking outside the Army. The mission here seems too small for me now, after this week. After actually helping people." He thought longer. "There are bad people out there, Jack. The ones behind Panama Red, that island with the kids. Whoever sent in the black helicopter that attacked the village. Whoever funded the people that tried to hunt us down in the jungle. We both know they weren't PDF. You said it yourself.

"Where is all that coordination and money coming from? Where is it going? Why? Why would someone have those levels of resources and choose to do evil?

"I can't live in a world where they go unpunished. I can't sleep at night knowing they are out there. If

I stay in the Army, I'll eventually get another field assignment, doing security background checks in the meantime. The next field assignment will be like the last one: low-level stuff.

"On top of that, the Army is full of holes. The entire MI branch is compromised. Between officers like Crostino who only care about their career, to people like Cruz and whoever else is leaking things…" Lasher trailed off. "I have enough leave saved up to get me past the obligation date. I'm done as of now. I'm going to Mariana's funeral, and I'm not coming back."

Williams smiled. "Sounds like your mind's made up."

Lasher realized that it was. "Jack, you are a better soldier than I gave you credit for."

Williams continued smiling, looking over. "On that, sir, we finally agree."

OFFICE

When they arrived at Thomasito's house, they were met as returning heroes, the entire neighborhood coming out to welcome them, clapping as the car stopped and they disembarked. It was quite a heartwarming display.

Sofia ran out of the car and to her mom and dad for a big family hug. The other children were embraced by others in the neighborhood. Lasher and Williams explained what had happened to the big crowd. Many people vowed to help find the other children's homes. The whole thing was the best Lasher or Williams had felt in a long time.

After a couple hours, they departed, starting the half-hour drive back to Fort Clayton, the Army base.

Lasher kept smiling. "That's how I want to spend my life, Jack."

Williams nodded, understanding. "Yep, I get it. I don't know how you are going to do it, but I get it.

The Army—really, any of these systems, even law enforcement—have a different agenda. If you figure it out, I'd be happy to join you."

Lasher nodded. This was a big step for Williams, he realized. Maybe more of an epiphany than Lasher's own realization. Williams was a company man, happy to be in the system. Being able to even contemplate something else was a significant step forward.

"Well, today isn't all rainbows and bunnies. We're going to be in front of Crostino in about twenty minutes." Lasher allowed the realization to set in, letting go of the feeling of deep satisfaction at returning Sofia to her family.

Williams clearly went through the same emotions. "When are you going to tell her?" Meaning, when would Lasher let her know he planned on resigning his commission?

Lasher thought for a few moments. "Let's get her up to speed on everything first, then I'll tell her."

They drove in silence the rest of the way, eventually clearing the MP station to enter Fort Clayton. Williams took them directly to the company day building. It was in the corner of the base, away from the main administrative complex. It looked different from the surrounding building on the base. It didn't have a first floor; instead, it was up on concrete pylons about ten feet off the ground.

It was around lunchtime, so most of the personnel

would be on their lunch break, but Crostino would be in her office. She rarely ever took lunch. They parked the car and went into the building, walking past cubicles and work areas. There were a few people here and there.

When they got to Crostino's office, the door was open. She was sitting at her desk facing the door, head down, working on something. She was tall, wearing pressed green Army fatigues.

Lasher knocked on the open door. "Good afternoon, ma'am."

She looked up and did a double take, taking a moment to recognize who it was. "Well, look at this. My two wandering gypsies have returned home." She motioned for them to enter. "You two look terrible."

Lasher had forgotten just how much had happened since he last saw her. Both he and Williams were beaten up with a lot of bruises and scratches. He had shaved his beard and cut his hair back to regulation. Both he and Williams had lost probably ten pounds, and their clothes, while cleaned yesterday at the hospital, were torn and still stained with blood.

They both entered and stood in front of Crostino's desk, not exactly at attention or at ease, as they were in civilian clothes, but close enough to show less formal respect.

"Close the door, and please sit down." She gestured

to the two chairs in front of the desk.

Williams stepped back and closed the door, joining Lasher in the opposite chair.

Crostino looked at them hard. "I'm not sure what to make of all of this. I suppose to start things off, the good news is that I received word from the DEA that their objectives in-country were met. They extended a thank you to this command for our participation and liaison activities."

Lasher nodded.

"However"—Crostino went from neutral to irritated—"they also sent a hospital bill for two agents, Lasher, that you beat up."

Lasher nodded.

Crostino looked at him, waiting.

He looked back with no expression, waiting.

Eventually, she said, "I expect there is more to the story?"

Lasher tilted his head, careful to hold eye contact and not look away. "Yes, ma'am, I would expect so."

She waited for a few beats more, then, "We can come back to that, I suppose. I also received a report that a PDF substation was attacked. Near your assigned condo, Wiliams."

Williams had about the same look as Lasher. "Yes, ma'am. I have heard the same thing."

Something replaced her irritation, but it was hard

to tell what. "Why don't one of you provide me with your report then." She put her pen down and leaned back in her chair.

Lasher responded immediately. "During the DEA raid at *Los Bravos,* we came across some female hostages. They told us that a bus with children had left earlier on their way to the farm, where the DEA planned on attacking the next day. We intercepted the children before it could get there. We informed the DEA SAIC, and he gave us the green light."

He turned to Williams, who nodded.

She looked between the two for a moment. "Then Williams, why were you involved? And why did you take an analyst from another company with you?"

Williams started to respond, but Lasher spoke first. "Ma'am, when you recalled Cruz, you took my planned CIC coordinator, so I borrowed Williams. We took an analyst to work with him, strictly off-mission, as support since we would have the opportunity for real-time battlefield intelligence gathering. I wanted a strategic set of eyes with us."

Williams nodded again as if that was precisely what he was going to say.

Crostino looked at Lasher, her face expressionless.

He could see wheels turning behind her eyes, then the look of resolve crossed her face.

"Okay," she said. Then again, "Okay. That seems to

cover everything, and we end up with a thank you from the DEA. We lost a soldier to a panther attack. Not much anyone can say about that. It was done while rescuing some kidnapped kids. Decision support in real time. It was a good call."

She made a look of resolution and picked her pen back up, ready to dismiss them.

"There is one more thing, ma'am," Lasher said, still seated.

She looked at him, a little annoyed. "What?"

"I would like to take some of my saved-up leave after the funeral."

"I can give you three days for bereavement." She was back to reading and marking up whatever report she had in front of her, not looking up.

"Thank you, ma'am. I would also like to use my personal leave. I have sixty days."

Crostino looked back up, her hand in mid-notation. "That's fine, Chief." Looking back down, too busy for more interaction, she said a curt "Dismissed."

Lasher and Williams both stood, said "Ma'am" each, opened the door, and walked out.

Once back outside the building, Williams stopped. "You're going to try and out-process from Fort Meade, aren't you?"

Lasher smiled and put his hand out. "Jack, it has

truly been a pleasure." They shook hands. "I'll look you up once I figure out what I am going to do."

They shook hands a second time, then Lasher turned to walk away.

"Where are you going? I can give you a lift," Williams said.

"Thanks, Jack, no. I'm just going to walk back to the barracks. It's not far. I'll get the travel schedule for Mariana's body and fly back with it."

They each put a hand up to indicate goodbye.

FUNERAL

L asher stood next to the casket that held Mariana. It was a cold January morning in Maryland, near Washington, D.C. Snow flurries were in the air, blowing in the breeze, not sticking to anything once reaching the ground. Everything was brown, the opposite of Panama this time of year. Snow was piled in a few places here and there from a prior storm, little left from where it had been shoveled except a dirty black residue.

He stood saluting as the two-soldier honor guard folded the flag that had been on top of the casket. It was a small cemetery. There were not that many people here. Mariana's mother and brother, six or seven friends, a couple of cemetery personnel, a priest, and the three soldiers, including Lasher.

As Lasher stood there, he ran through some things in his head. He would try to talk to Deputy Director Wolf, Mariana's mother, after the service. Wolf was an impressive-looking woman with an unmistakable resemblance to her daughter; the two could have been mistaken for sisters.

Eventually, the service ended. Lasher shook hands with the two soldiers in the honor guard and told them they were dismissed. He remained by the gravesite to allow the family and friends to exchange condolences and hugs. After a few moments of that, Wolf made eye contact with him and headed over. He saw, back by the car park, two men that looked like personal security for Wolf.

Wolf walked over. "Lieutenant," she said, addressing Lasher, seeing the single silver bar on his class A dress uniform. "Thank you for escorting Sarah back here. I understand you were with her when the accident happened." She extended her hand, and Lasher took it. It was a solid, firm handshake.

"Yes, ma'am. I am sorry for your loss." He let the rank confusion go. There was no point in worrying about correcting a grieving mother on a trivial matter, given the context. "She was helping to rescue four Panamanian children captured by Columbian *Narcotraficante.*"

Wolf held eye contact. "I received a letter from her company commander. He tried to explain the situation to me, but it did not completely make sense."

Lasher nodded. "Yes, ma'am. We were reacting in real time to intelligence in a coordinated in-country operation with the DEA."

Something clicked behind Wolf's eyes.

Lasher continued. "A group of the *Narcotraficante* was taking the children to a location that would be under fire. We intercepted them; we were working our way back out of the jungle."

She continued to look hard at Lasher. He couldn't make out the expression and started to feel a little uncomfortable.

Stand here and take it. You recruited Mariana; she was under your command. The least you can do is give her mother closure.

After a few more beats of holding eye contact, Wolf asked, "Was this the raid at *Los Bravos?*" It looked like she was trying to connect the events, piece them together in her head to get a complete understanding.

Lasher was taken aback. "How could you know that?"

The locations of the DEA activities were classified. Yes, Wolf had Top Secret access, but her job was a lot bigger than the trivial dealings in Panama; the DIA operated globally.

She looked at Lasher differently. "You were the Army liaison?"

Lasher was now confused. "Yes, ma'am."

"Lieutenant—" she started to say.

Lasher decided to correct her. It seemed the conversation had shifted; he didn't want to later have her confused about his rank. "Ma'am," he interjected, "I'm a W3, Chief Warrant Officer. Didn't want you confused."

"Thank you, Chief. That helps some. I couldn't figure out how you hadn't made captain yet, but that explains it." Someone of Lasher's age still only an O2 would have suggested he was a screwup, unpromotable.

She continued. "Chief, let me finish the process of grieving my daughter. We have a wake at my house now. Can you meet me at three o'clock today?"

"Yes, ma'am."

"Where are you staying?"

"I'm at the Capital Hilton."

"Perfect. We can meet at my club. It's just a block away from there on 1135 16ᵗʰ Street. It's a private club. When you go in, tell the desk you are there to see me. I'll let them know you are coming."

They shook hands. She started to leave, then turned back around. "So you know, the *Los Bravos* raid was my project. I'll give you more details when we talk."

Lasher took a cab back to his hotel. He changed from his uniform to comfortable civilian clothes, blue jeans, and a T-shirt. He had a light jacket and running shoes.

Not exactly private club, meet the DIA deputy director attire, but it's all I have.

He arrived at the club a few minutes early. It was just a block away down 16th Street. The White House was several blocks the other way, clearly visible at the end of the broad street.

The desk at the club was expecting him when he asked for Wolf. They told him he needed to wear a sports coat at a minimum. Him not having one, they gave him an ill-fitting yellow sports coat with the club logo on it to wear. He traded his windbreaker for it at the coat check.

He was told there was a lounge up a sizeable ornate staircase, and to his left. He headed up the stairs and saw Wolf at a small table in a large room with a mahogany bar running along one side of it. There were a few other people scattered here and there, a barman behind the bar and two waiters working the room. Wolf's table was by a window looking out on 16th Street.

As he approached, she made a motion to the chair on the other side of the table. She had a drink in front of her, something clear and brown, scotch or whisky.

"Can I have them bring you anything?" she asked.

Lasher almost asked for a beer but thought better of it. "No, thank you," he returned instead.

Wolf made a motion to the bartender. "Another round. He'll have what I am having."

Lasher looked at her, uncertain.

"We're going to toast Sarah."

"Yes, ma'am." No argument from him.

A man brought the drinks over, and she held hers up. "To Sarah. My headstrong little girl."

They clinked glasses, and both threw back the alcohol. Whatever it was, it burned on the way down, but it was the smoothest shot Lasher had ever had.

"I looked you up on my way here," Wolf said stoically.

"Yes, ma'am." Lasher wasn't sure what else to say.

"You have a decade in service. Joined the Army at eighteen as an infantryman. Got recruited out of Basic to join a Ranger battalion. Dropped into Grenada in eighty-three. Awarded the bronze star for bravery under enemy fire. You carried a fellow Ranger ten miles from your drop zone. He had busted his knees on landing. You fought your way out.

"Applied for warrant officer right after Grenada, got accepted, changed your MOS to 97B, counterintelligence agent. Did a tour in Libya, received a Silver Star for bravery under enemy fire. You helped after the bombing, then were assigned as an operative in Panama.

"You speak seven languages and completed your undergraduate degree while in the service."

"Yes, ma'am."

"I just have one question for you."

"Yes, ma'am?"

"Was my daughter's sacrifice worth it." It didn't come out as a question.

Lasher thought for a few moments. "No, ma'am. No sacrifice is ever worth it, and your daughter was a good soldier. However, that said, she would tell you that she did the right thing and that she would do it again. If it could have been me instead of her, I would have made that trade instantly.

"But here we are. Four Panamanian children now get a chance at a regular life. She saved them from hell on Earth."

Wolf nodded, apparently hearing what she needed to hear. She motioned to the bartender, making a circle with her finger. Another round.

After the drinks came, she asked, "Chief, do you believe in coincidence?"

He looked back at her. Her eyes were clear and sharp. The deputy director held her liquor well.

"Do you?" he asked.

Wolf smiled. "Not today." Leaning forward, she said, "We have been looking for someone to head up operations in our southern theater. Field ops, someone to get the work done.

"*Los Bravos,* it wasn't what you were told it was. We have a major threat in the region we are working to counter." She lowered her voice. "The whole region has holes. You know what I mean?"

Lasher nodded, he did. He had come to the same conclusion. The undercover assignments, safe houses, coordination with the PDF, and other entities.

"You don't know this, Chief." Wolf's voice returned to normal. "Sarah called me after you asked her to help. She was very excited about the opportunity. She looked up to you, more than you may know. She told me about her arrival, how you helped make sure she got a fair shake. How you took care of a situation for her."

Lasher nodded; he wasn't really sure where Wolf was going. While what she said was true, he didn't like the idea of getting credit for something that any decent person would have done in his position.

"Come work for me," Wolf said, her eyes blazing. "We've been looking for someone to lead this new team. I have interviewed close to two hundred people. It can't be a coincidence that we are talking. The requirements for the job are experience as a field grade officer in an intelligence discipline, real fieldwork experience, and an undergraduate degree.

"The position is a GS-13. You'll keep your time in service. It will transfer with you."

Wolf paused, clearly not finished speaking. "Let's make my daughter's sacrifice mean something."

Lasher looked out the window at the street, clearing his thoughts. "Your timing is better than you might think." He smiled a thin smile, looking back at her. "Let me be honest. I have already decided to resign from my commission. I want to spend my time helping people. I want to directly contribute to making things better. To address corruption, help the oppressed, bring justice."

She smiled. "You'll get a lot closer to that working for me than the Army. The position is based out of Fort Huachuca. You know it; you attended your MI training there. You will have complete operational control. Limited oversight. I'll give you objectives, you'll fulfill them.

"I'm not a micromanager. A lot of what you do will be up to you." She finished her pitch.

Lasher leaned back, really trying to take in the conversation. Things were moving a lot faster than he thought they would. His original plan was to spend time figuring out what he wanted to do next.

"I am inclined to say yes. Can you give me a day to think about it?"

She smiled again. "I can give you two days."

SHARP

L asher gave the sports coat back at the coat check; they returned his windbreaker. There was a box with miscellaneous clothing items in it. He asked about it and was told it was sort of lost and found. After some negotiating, he was able to get a scarf from the box, after which he walked out the front of the building.

The day was chilly; the sky was gray. The sun would be setting in about an hour. It would turn too cold for his thin jacket then; the scarf would help, but he would still be uncomfortable. He looked left and right, realizing that he didn't have anywhere to go and had nothing to do for the first time in a long time.

He turned left, heading back in the direction of his hotel, walking past it up to K Street. He crossed over and headed west. The Farragut North Subway stop was a block and a half down the street. He walked to it, then past it, temporarily flirting with the idea of getting on the train and going somewhere, the cold weather changing his mind. He kept going, eventually coming to the intersection of K Street and Pennsylvania Avenue, a big traffic circle roundabout.

To his left was George Washington University Law School, to his right 22nd Street. There were a lot of restaurants and bars to the right. He went right with the thought of getting a drink, but nothing jumped out, and the idea of sitting in a bar by himself did not hold much interest. He turned and followed Pennsylvania Avenue west and north.

After a few blocks, he came to Rock Creek Park. It was a decent wooded area with a stream running through it, a running trail, and benches here and there. The Embassy of Qatar was on the corner. He walked into the park and found a bench far enough in, with no one else around, where he could see the stream. There were small coverings of ice here and there, but the water still flowed.

He sat down on the bench, not really thinking about anything. Also, thinking about everything. But nothing specific. The DIA offer was almost too good to be true, almost as if the universe had groomed him for that specific opportunity, everything from his training to meeting Mariana's mother, Deputy Director Wolf.

He couldn't think of a reason not to take it, but he wasn't sure it was what he wanted either. It sounded like it was a lot more freedom to pursue the matters he thought necessary. Indeed, better pay and the thought of preserving his military time and having it rolled into a federal government retirement plan, well, it had its merits.

What would Grandpa say? he wondered briefly.

Don't start chasing shadows again. What would you *say? That's the better question.*

Lasher was starting to allow himself some more profound thoughts when a man and woman walked up to him.

The man was a tough-looking Hispanic with a military haircut. Older than Lasher by a good ten years or so, he had a dangerous look to him with his black leather jacket. His hands were thick and scarred. The woman was wearing a red dress; she must have been freezing because it looked like an expensive party dress, but in the cold, it was clear that was all she was wearing.

The man and woman exchanged glances, the woman nodding.

"*Pardon me,*" the man said in Spanish, "*do you speak Spanish? We are lost and do not speak English very well.*"

"*I speak Spanish,*" Lasher said back. Something wasn't right with these two.

The woman produced a big paper folding map from somewhere. "*Can you show us where we are on this map? We need to get back to my friend's house in*

Georgetown."

It didn't feel right, but she stepped forward with the map before he could say anything. The map completely blocked his view. Something happened, and all of a sudden, the man had hit him in the head and got a rope around his neck. Lasher moved quickly; he could get a hand up under the rope, the scarf he had on helping with the leverage.

Just like the Wargandi. I'm sick of ropes.

The man was strong. He pulled Lasher over and got him up on his knees, standing behind him with control of the noose.

The woman's demeanor changed. She sat down on the bench in front of Lasher. "Chief Dirk Lasher," she presented very professionally. "You have caused me a lot of problems; do you know that?"

She paused for him to respond. He didn't.

"Hernando, loosen the rope. We're all friends here. For the moment, anyway."

Hernando did not loosen the rope.

"You are a hard man to find, Mr. Lasher. We almost had you a couple of times." She saw he still was having a hard time breathing. "Hernando! Loosen. The. Rope."

The noose was loosened a little; Lasher could more easily breathe and talk. He carefully moved his hand farther under, between the rope and his neck. He felt pretty confident he had enough of a grip he would be able to counteract the noose being tightened again.

"It was a shame about your young friend, the one who died. What was her name?"

Wait, I think she is suggesting that she has been behind the events in Panama. I'm going to take a guess here.

"You're the one behind the GBG." Lasher stated it firmly as if he had known all along. Of course, he wasn't sure. It was just a guess on his part.

The woman looked at the man behind him. "Oh, Hernando, this one is a smart one." Back to Lasher: "You cost me a month of the schedule."

"You cost me five DEA agents, two friends, and a good soldier. Not to mention all the innocent Panamanians you killed."

The DEA agents killed at Los Bravos, Thomasito's two friends, the Wargandi village, and Mariana.

The woman flushed; her face turned red at the cheeks. It was a reaction to happiness, he thought.

"Good! Now we are getting somewhere! Yes! But those lives were in your hands, not mine. You should have just stayed drunk on your home-brewed beer and let the PDF arrest you for spying in their country. Then your friends would still be alive!"

"Lady, do you have a point you want to make? Otherwise, let's get on with this."

She smiled a big smile. "No point." She looked around, contemplating something. "Hernando, cut his clothes off."

Lasher had no idea where that would go, but he was done. Moving as quickly as he could, he pulled the noose over his head, getting it off, pushing back on the man behind him, then diving forward and rolling onto his feet.

The woman sat forward, excited. "Yes! Oh good, finally a fighter." Tapping her foot with anticipation.

The man, Hernando, reached around his back. Lasher guessed he was going for a knife. Not waiting, he took a step toward the woman on the bench and landed a right cross, as hard as he could, directly on her jaw. It felt like something gave way, her jaw or maybe some of her teeth. Either way, she was knocked out, slumping backward with the force of the blow.

"You shouldn't have done that!" Hernando said in English, a look of horror on his face, producing a big hunting knife, well made, with a partial curve to the blade. It was a mean-looking knife.

If you get into a knife fight, you're going to get cut, Lasher remembered from the first week of Ranger training. The trick was not to worry about superficial wounds but instead neutralize the knife as quickly as possible. Either disable the user or get control of the weapon as fast as you could.

Hernando was in a low fighting stance.

Lasher was in his first position Kenpo stance, but then he dropped his guard, standing up straight, looking Hernando in the eye. "They call you Hernando. Let me guess, Mexican Special Forces?"

Hernando smiled, not relaxing his stance as Lasher had. "A little of this, a little of that."

"I just want to be clear. You and this lady were behind everything I went through the past couple of weeks?"

"Yes, friend. And more."

A wave of anger so deep and so primal swelled up in Lasher he literally saw red, his sightline adopting the hue. More adrenaline was flowing through him than he had ever known, fueling a rage that he had been suppressing since his grandfather was killed a decade ago.

All of it came out; he became rage incarnate.

Something must have changed on Lasher's face. Hernando looked taken aback briefly, then charged, the knife in front with his right hand—a fast, direct attack.

Lasher pivoted the blow, his scarf now in both hands, using it to counter the knife thrust.

Hernando spun around after the initial attack missed, swinging the knife at eye level, aiming for Lasher's face.

Lasher countered again, dropping the scarf and twisting to grab Hernando's knife hand, knocking the knife to the ground, and holding on to the hand. He bent it around backward, behind Hernando's back. The knife clattered to the ground, hit the path, then bounced into the dead grass.

In practice, the move would be to lift the arm, giving him total control of Hernando, the pain from the handhold unbearable. But this wasn't practice. Instead of stopping at the control point, he continued to raise Hernando's hand and arm. Too far, then he hit down as hard as he could, breaking the arm above the elbow and at the wrist.

Hernando screamed.

Lasher thought it was a good scream, full of real pain from a tough man.

Hernando fell to his knees. Lasher kicked the arm, hard, where it had broken, using his heel to further offset the fracture. The bottom of the arm bone broke out of the skin. Hernando screamed again, a more resounding, more agonizing wail.

He fell to the ground face first.

Lasher walked over to him, rolling him over with a kick to the ribs, looking him in the eye once he could focus. Hernando's eyes were wild with fear and pain. He was trying to say something, but Lasher didn't care.

Lasher raised his foot. Hernando got out the word

"No. Pl…" and was gone, stomped out of existence in the cold park as the sun set, an end to both the day and the man.

Lasher sat back down on the bench next to Sharp. Streetlights were starting to come on, not near where he was, but he could see the back of the Qatar Embassy and the streets beyond. It was getting cold, but Lasher didn't feel it.

He picked up Sharp, put her over his shoulder to carry her, and walked to the embassy. When he got there, he banged on the door.

A man answered, opening the door. "I'm sorry, sir, we close at five. Are you a Qatari National?" The man looked at Lasher then the woman on his shoulder.

"No, sir. I require aid. This woman is my prisoner. I need to use your phone, please."

He let Lasher in, directing him to a front foyer with several chairs, a couch, and a phone. Lasher dumped Sharp unceremoniously on the couch and picked up the phone, reaching into his pocket for Wolf's private phone number and then dialing it.

"That was fast," Wolf said when she answered.

Lasher didn't even bother worrying about how she knew it was him.

"I'm in," he said.

"That's great news. When can you start?"

"I already started. We need to clean up a KIA in Rock Creek Park before the local police find him. And I have, I believe, the head of the GBG, the person in charge of southern operations at least."

"You're at the Qatar Embassy?"

"Yes."

"I'll send someone over. The challenge will be 'We're looking for a friend of ours.'"

"I know it," Lasher replied, noting the irony.

This new job is starting the same way the old one ended.

With no joy in his voice, Lasher said, "We're all friends here, *amigo,*" as the line went dead.

The End.

AUTHORS CLOSING NOTE

I hoped you enjoyed reading Panama Red.

If you did, leaving an honest review helps others discover the book.

You can use this link to go directly to the review page for this book:

https://www.amazon.com/review/create-review/?asin=B09CTT1Q8S

Dirk will return in *Storm Fire* the next exciting book in the series, in 2022.

Writing this book was an interesting experience, different from other books I have written.

For *Panama Red*, I did more 'remembering' than

'creating'.

Each of the set pieces in the book is based on real-world events that I lived.

Of course, the context is entirely different.

But, the PDF station raid, the helicopter attack on *Los Bravos*, the dangerous pursuit into the deep jungle all happened in about the same way as described in the book and at about the same time as described.

Oh, and yes, we did save a baby panther.

Made in the USA
Columbia, SC
01 October 2021